# Unfettered Wings

**Sana Munir** has a master's degree in Mass Communication Theory and Research from the University of the Punjab, Lahore. The degree earned her two gold medals at the provincial and national levels.

She has taught International Communication and Feminist Film Theory at her alma mater, Lahore College for Women University. Sana has also freelanced for various prominent magazines in Pakistan. Her interest in feminism is embedded in her writings, both journalistic and now literary, in the form of her debut collection of short stories, *Unfettered Wings*. To Sana, feminism is not a mere school of thought or ideology but an entire way of living, rooted in essential moral principles of equality, humanity, acceptance and justice.

She believes she is hereditarily gifted by her father—a writer, teacher and poet—and whatever writing skills she has been able to develop over the years, are because of him.

Sana blogs at sanamunirblog.wordpress.com

# Unfettered Wings

*Extraordinary Stories of Ordinary Women*

## SANA MUNIR

Published by
Rupa Publications India Pvt. Ltd 2018
7/16, Ansari Road, Daryaganj
New Delhi 110002

*Sales centres:*
Allahabad Bengaluru Chennai
Hyderabad Jaipur Kathmandu
Kolkata Mumbai

Copyright © Sana Munir 2018

This is a work of fiction. Names, characters, places and incidents are either the product of the author's imagination or are used fictitiously and any resemblance to any actual person, living or dead, events or locales is entirely coincidental.

All rights reserved.
No part of this publication may be reproduced, transmitted, or stored in a retrieval system, in any form or by any means, electronic, mechanical, photocopying, recording or otherwise, without the prior permission of the publisher.

ISBN: 978-93-5304-054-3

First impression 2018

10 9 8 7 6 5 4 3 2 1

Printed at Thomson Press India Ltd., Faridabad

This book is sold subject to the condition that it shall not, by way of trade or otherwise, be lent, resold, hired out, or otherwise circulated, without the publisher's prior consent, in any form of binding or cover other than that in which it is published.

*For Rafia*
*Sister, friend, confidante*

# Contents

Farida / 1
*An unforgettable monsoon in 1947*

Reema / 22
*The keeper of secrets*

Maria / 43
*The wanton one*

Summi / 70
*The soldier's wife*

Habiba / 88
*The girl with topaz eyes*

Nazia / 117
*In pursuit of happiness*

Saima / 142
*On the trail of a dead bride*

Beena / 169
*Love me like Shah Rukh Khan*

Meera / 183
*Professor Crank*

Eeman / 199
*Keeping faith*

Acknowledgements / 215

# Farida
*An unforgettable monsoon in 1947*

Rust-coloured dust rose from the ground until the entire landscape was enveloped in cloud-like formations. The cousins, brothers, uncles and friends, who now waited at the train station, had been sensing the vibration of the coal-fueled vehicle from the time when it was half a kilometre away. They had glued their eyes to the horizon for a sight of the reddish dust to rise—a sign of the train cutting through the thick monsoon air. The train had finally reached its destination safely. It had halted in the midst of a crowd which was chattering in loud voices and waiting in anticipation on both sides of the dusty tracks. They had come to receive the torn chapters of their filial history—those who had boarded the train from Patiala to go to Lahore.

Those who had already departed from Patiala had known that their journey would not last for more than two hours on the train. They had packed the bare essentials, as if they were going on a family vacation and would return home in a matter of days. They carried money, jewellery, clothes and rations to last a few days. Some had been overly cautious and had buried their valuables back home in a hand-dug pit, so secretively in the darkness of the night, that even a son didn't know where his father had hidden the treasure. Electricity was a thing of the future, so oil lamps, kerosene lanterns and candles had been trusted while doing the job.

Some of them had been prepared beforehand, but some had to flee in such a hurry that the stoves were left burning, the earthen pot of curry, boiling, and the flatbread, burning black. Some had boarded the train with the complete headcount they had had as they set foot from home, while some had lost women to rapists, children to sodomizers, and men to murderers. They were defectors for the ethnocentric-minded. No part of the subcontinent could be torn to be a separate entity; those who didn't want to live in the motherland, had to choose death.

Laal had weighed his options very carefully. Just twenty-four hours before boarding the train from Patiala to Lahore, he was still unsure which one of his children or grandchildren shall be left behind. If it weren't for his stoicism, this would not be a story worth telling. He was a withering man, going into his seventies, who had decided that his two sons would leave for Lahore.

'I will stay back,' the older son, Ashfaq, had announced.

Laal was pained, but he decided to put up a brave face.

'Either we all leave or we all stay behind,' he stated grimly but decisively. The rest of the family had hung their heads over their bosoms, as if they were being taken to the gallows.

## Farida

The meeting was being held in the large common room of the joint-family house, which was deliberately kept dark because of the horror of the riots. Those homes that gave off even the tiniest sign of a communal gathering of sorts, were giving out an unspoken invitation to the rioters who were always ready to annihilate. It had been heard the same morning that the neighbouring village in the north had been torched. The mob would lock the doors from the outside so that no one could escape, and set fire to the houses. The sad thing was, everyone was doing it to each other. Farida felt a sting on her arm, as a spark from the coal casket of Laal's hookah came flying towards her. She slapped her arm, thinking an ant must have torn a chunk off her flesh, but found a bit of timber instead. It crumbled in between her thumb and finger when she held it. The scene in front of her eyes was a grave one, although she had very little idea of what was going on.

Laal's family sat huddled on the charpoys inside. The babies had nestled into the softest cushions of their mother's fleshy bodies, while the older children stood dumbfounded, trying to make sense of whatever monstrosity the grown-ups were talking about. All that the kids could picturize, though, were hazy images of a train ride being planned. But there was something… something unusual about the way the grown-ups talked about it. They talked about swords, canes and fire on the train. The children could only imagine a carnival. The talks were long and winding, filled with sighs of dismay. Farida, the eldest among the children, had been sitting throughout the session, getting desperate, by the minute, to come to the part that explained the fireworks on the train. That would be some train trip through the monsoon!

The days were hot and damp in the midst of August. Hence, being locked indoors was making it very overwhelming for people who were forced to inhale an excess of carbon dioxide, along with fear, horror, dismay, helplessness and emotional turmoil. A loyal lantern had been burning since the morning because the women had been too scared to open the windows. The flame inside the glass casing flickered every now and then, and the movement made the shadows of every being in the room, dance in different directions. Farida had been looking at the patterns of the shadows. The biggest one was of Ashfaq, a large man with a muscly torso. He towered above everyone else in the family.

At her age, Farida had not quite understood what repercussions her father's staying back in Patiala might have for him or the family, and in particular, for her. To the little girl, it seemed to be the most selfless choice to sacrifice the idea of a holiday for the sake of tending to the buffaloes, the house and the land. She was young but not naïve to not notice her uncle's bowed head as the conversation went on. Her mother had huddled together Farida's two baby brothers and brought them closer to herself. She yanked her head up in protest when her husband had spoken of his choice, but immediately afterwards, had put it back in a position of submission.

Laal had chosen to argue with Ashfaq. 'I cannot leave the land untended. Not for them to reap my harvest.' When he wanted to make a point, Ashfaq's voice could have the audacity of a lion's roar.

*Farida*

'The land is not more important than your life!' Laal did not have a thunderous tone to match his son's, but he had stood up as he spoke and had tapped the floor hard with his walking stick to make up for the lack of intonation of his voice.

'I have promised Qasim and the rest. I will join you people as soon as the chaos is over,' Ashfaq replied in a matter-of-fact tone. The old man was left with no choice but to sit down. Farida looked at her father with some consternation. She was the eldest child in her family and, being the daughter, had been made to understand that after Ma, she was responsible for her little brothers. Even Uncle Mushtaq's kids were younger than her.

She suddenly felt a surge of responsibility towards her father. She couldn't just leave him alone. But she had witnessed how her grandfather had been turned down and although she had every intention to offer her company to her father, she still felt a sense of giddiness gushing through her body, thinking of a train ride. Ever since she had heard about the newly installed tracks and the railway system in her village, as well as the uniformed guard who would march down to the platform every day, Farida had been eager to visit the place and ride the train. The station was three kilometres away from where she lived, and since her village was a quiet place, the hoot of the siren and the chuk-chuk of the engine always reached her ears, fascinating her. So, despite her increasing feeling of protectiveness that did not want to let her father stay alone, the anticipation of the forthcoming vacation to Lahore turned out to be much stronger.

Her only worry was whether she looked good enough to go to the city of the rich. Laal, whom she called Abbaji like the elders, had shaved all her hair when summer had started, because Ma was tired of pulling out the lice and nits from her mane. Abbaji had warned her that if she didn't stop playing with the girls in the street who gave her the infection, he would never let her hair grow back. She had implored and wept, but Abbaji was rigid. He said it was possible for him to do it now but next year, she would be a big girl. So, as bald as the moon, she only had the green-and-yellow kurti to suffice for the trip to Lahore. The white lattha salwar was also good enough.

While Farida contemplated the most difficult decision of her life, Ashfaq had closed his arguments.

In Farida's father's books, the meeting had ended. Abbaji would take them all to Lahore, and Ashfaq would stay behind. He had grabbed his spear from the narrow slit in the wall above the door. Farida saw her Pa cover his head and face with the cotton shawl he wore around his neck, and grasp the spear so tight as if someone might snatch it from him. The fastened-up door was gently opened and he disappeared into the night, not looking back even once.

Abbaji signalled Farida to shut the door. Her mother had managed to put one of the babies to sleep. The other was beginning to wail for milk. Farida noticed fear in her mother's eyes. Although she would not understand for a long time why her Pa had gone out with a spear in his hand, her mother's wet eyes had conveyed that something wasn't quite right.

Abbaji got up from the charpoy, squatted in a corner with his staff in one hand and rested his head on the other. He had no idea whether his son would even return home that night.

## Farida

Farida didn't know what to do or say, so she tried to figure out things on her own. Everyone was sad, so something bad was happening or was expected to happen. Uncle Mushtaq had not spoken the entire night. He was comforting his wife, Asiya, who was gently sobbing. Was she crying for Pa? Farida didn't understand what was going on. She looked at her mother, who was sombre and silent. They both knew Ashfaq was a fighter; they needn't worry about him.

Ashfaq was a man of strength. His day job was to work in the field, look after the cattle and irrigate the land. He had begun as a young helper to his father, working on the family land. Mushtaq was the idle one. He had never liked hard work. The ploughing made him cranky, and the obstinate moss, algae and weeds were irksome to him. Hence, Ashfaq had single-handedly taken over the little piece of land they owned, to produce grain for their home as well as make enough profit from sales to meet the other expenditures of the household. However, Mushtaq could not be allowed to loiter, so Laal and Ashfaq had used their savings to set up a small candy store for him. The store was as humble as the environs it was set in—a small three-by-three-feet cabin outside the family house with an open front, a wooden plank straightened out to make a counter across the two walls on either side, and clay canisters filled with candied carrot strips and apple chunks, aniseeds coated with a colourful, sugary paste, and granola bars made with rice crispies, peanuts and raisins.

All of these were prepared by his wife at home, and his loyal customers were the kids from around the neighbourhood. It was not the kind of business that would bring prosperity to a household, but nonetheless, it kept him busy. Mushtaq was lazy, but very respectful towards his elder brother. He had always addressed his older sibling as Pa, which was a colloquial version of 'brother'. When Farida was learning to talk, the only name she had heard ringing in the house for her father, was 'Pa,' and she, too, picked it up. It stuck with her, and Ashfaq had no objection. That night, when she saw Uncle Mushtaq submissively hang his head as Pa thundered, she felt more responsible for her family than ever.

Farida heard her grandfather and mother whisper to each other to go to sleep, for they had both promised to stay up for Pa. However, neither could close their eyes and slumped in different corners of the room, staring at the walls. The kids were yawning and murmuring their lullabies to themselves, since they could sense that their mothers were too fatigued to sing them anything. Farida had stretched out on the ground, just close to the door through which her father had walked out. Although she had vowed to wait for him like her Abbaji and mother, her eyes refused to cooperate with her plan. She dozed off on the floor.

Later, she had a very blurry but unforgettable memory of opening her eyes a little, sometime during the night—her father had come home; his spear was coated in a thick layer of blood. The blood was not dripping but had coagulated around the spear. His clothes had the same stains of red which he always got when he slaughtered a goat to commemorate Bakra Eid every year. She sat up, worried, thinking her Pa was hurt, but then she saw Abbaji sit next to him while he removed the shawl that veiled his face. She saw her father hide his face behind his huge hands, which had become rough because of farming. There was a whiff of burnt cloth, kerosene and ashes in the room. Laal slid his feeble arm over Ashfaq's shoulders, which shook with a rhythmic movement. Considering Abbaji had it all covered, she went back to sprawl on the floor and let sleep overcome her.

The next morning was no different than the previous night. Everyone was quiet, but their faces were an amalgam of emotive disturbance. They had to leave in the afternoon train, which meant they needed an hour and a half to walk down to the platform with the kids. Laal had been undoing the seams of his cotton vest. Both his daughters-in-law were busy packing the food rations into waterproof, jute sacks, to be hidden like a pirate's treasure in a hole dug in the common room. The grains, ghee and palm sugar were hard-earned and could not be left for thieves. Almost everyone believed they would come back for their land, cattle and rations. Even if they couldn't stay, their possessions would have to be kept in a safe place for a possible use later.

Farida felt useless in the chaos around her. Uncle Mushtaq was distributing the candy from his store to the young ones in the neighbourhood. His clientele had crowded around him with both hands outstretched, trying to grab as much candy as they could in their small palms. They clutched the sticky carrots and apples so tight that sugary liquid oozed out from their hands. Uncle Mushtaq was giving away his merchandise, for the candies could not be stored and it was too much baggage to be carried along. Farida looked around the courtyard once again—her baby brothers and cousins had received their due share of Uncle Mushtaq's bounty as well.

Abbaji was still totally engrossed in pulling apart the seams of his vest, and Farida wondered why. Her mind raced through the accounts of the previous night; she was not sure whether seeing her father cry had happened in real or in a dream. She tiptoed inside the family room to have a dekko at the spear. It was tucked securely in its position. The smears of blood must have been wiped clean. There were footprints of ash on the floor. She was confused. She was too much of a coward to go ask her father about it, but there was one more person she could talk to. Actually, she could talk to that person anytime, about anything.

'Where is Pa, Abbaji?' Farida asked, sitting down on the floor beside her grandfather.

'At the field. Why?'

'Nothing. Everyone else is around…' She dodged her grandfather's puzzled eyes. He must have guessed that something was going on in her head.

'Well, everyone else around us is getting ready for the train that we have to board this afternoon. Are you ready for that, Farida?' He didn't quite make eye contact as he said this.

Her eyes shone so bright that before she could say anything, her grandfather's face broke into a little smile.

'Do you want to go without your father?' he asked. The question must have taken the shine away from her eyes because her grandfather, too, looked sad when he uttered it.

'We should all go,' she replied in her tiniest voice.

The old man had now started to sew something onto his vest.

*Farida*

'You know what Ashfaq and I were talking about last night, Farida?'

She sensed it was a trick question, so she played around. A girl of ten isn't as innocent as she looks.

'You were talking about going to Lahore.'

'Your father wants to stay behind. You heard him say that, too?'

She nodded gloomily.

'I want you to do something for me, Farida. You must be brave like your father when you do this little thing.' Abbaji was looking into her eyes. He had the kindest eyes ever, but his grave tone scared her a little.

'I am brave, Abbaji.' Her lips quivered slightly.

'Then you, my little girl, will have to tell your father that you won't leave without him.'

'But—'

A little frown had suddenly appeared on her face, and she was about to protest with all her might when her Abbaji stopped her midway.

'Just listen to me,' he said. 'You will leave with him. He will change that stubborn ox of his mind only if you react with equal obstinacy. You get me?'

His eyes were still boring into hers—searching his granddaughter's face, looking for an answer.

'Then who will look after the land?' she asked.

Laal looked relieved when he heard her answer, and said, 'I will.'

He went back to his sewing. She didn't ask him any more.

She sat there, watching him, thinking whether it was a good time to ask him about Pa crying, or which animal he had slaughtered last night whose blood had covered him and his spear. It was strange, since she had never seen him feel sorry for the goats, lambs or cows he slaughtered.

She was still thinking whether it was a good time to put forward these questions, when her grandfather prompted, 'Well?'

She almost blurted out the question, but then thinking better of it, clamped down her upper jaw over the lower one. 'Nothing,' she said, and rushed outside.

'Where to?' her mother called from behind.

'Fieeeeelds!' she shouted, without stopping to look at her.

She heard her mother's footsteps behind her, as if she was running to stop her, but Farida didn't look back. She could outrun her old lady any day of the week, and this day was special. She wanted to speak to Pa as soon as she could. The morning breeze was not quite as cool as it was every day. The horizon was looking dusty, as if a storm was on its way. There was a thin cloud of smoke rising a mile away from her village. It seemed as if someone had lit a huge bonfire the previous night. She recalled the ashes from Pa's feet.

'Aha!' she thought, so he has been having a bonfire at the neighbouring village. But why cry?

Her mind was racing just as fast as her feet. She ran across the street and the damp air entering her nostrils made her feel a little suffocated. Or maybe it was the nervous energy that filled her chest and stomach, which made her experience a bit

*Farida*

of apnea. Whatever it was, she still couldn't wait to see Pa. He usually left at dawn to do the watering and weeding, and by this time, he must be feeding the cattle.

After a few metres from where the humble-looking mud structures of the houses stood, the green fields started. Farmers from Farida's village took pride in their toil and weren't afraid of the peril at the fields. Wheat was their main crop, and just before the rains came in, the crop would be ready to be harvested like Ashfaq's was. As she ran towards the field, she could almost catch a glimpse of her land—golden in its entirety—all ready to be reaped in a couple of days' time. She expected to meet Prakash, Pa's loyal helper. He didn't have any land of his own but he worked as a farmer's mercenary, helping them during their harvest, the ploughing, and simply by keeping company to the cattle at night, in case any thieves tried to get lucky.

She could see a few heads bobbing up and down at the field. She was just a couple of yards away but slowed her pace. There was Pa, alright. But the three other men weren't familiar. She went closer. Her sight was partially blocked by a tall crop that stood between her and the others. Pa was held by his arms by two of those other men. The third was standing right in front of him. What she saw next, haunted her all her life. It was a scene she had not been able to obliterate either from her conscious memory or her subconscious mind. She saw her father being murdered. She saw the sheen of the dagger that was thrust inside his chest. She witnessed the exact number of times he was stabbed by the same man—three. She registered to her memory, the colour of her father's blood—it wasn't bright red like her mother's when she cut her finger, chopping vegetables—it was dark, like the blood of a bull.

She frantically looked around for help but there was no one. She could not forgive herself for a long time for not having the courage to go and fight off those men. It took her many years to realize that if she had gone to help her Pa, she would have been crushed, too. Her time had not come that day. But her father's had. After the third stab, they let her Pa fall to the ground. She wanted the men to go away so she could help him. Every moment seemed to stretch for eternity. She could have gone home and brought help, but she couldn't move.

In the heart of her heart, she never thought her Pa could die. The grandeur of his strength and the extent of his valour was such in her heart. But the truth is, her Pa couldn't make it. When the men finally started marching towards the village where the mud huts humbly stood, she made way through the golden crop to reach her father, who was lying on the ground, face down. His face was smeared with dust, and blood trickled from under him in a thin stream that seemed to water his beloved crops. The buffaloes were visibly disturbed; they made sounds which she would later hear during unpleasant dreams. She tried to turn him over to see if he could still make it with a few stitches over the stab wounds. She wasn't knowledgeable enough to know that it takes half a stab in the heart to make a body go lifeless.

It took her quite a lot of time to realize that Pa wasn't coming to life again. Who were the men who had killed her Pa so mercilessly? Did they come to kill all of Pa's friends? Will Qasim's children be orphaned, too? She thought of Uncle Mushtaq and her grandfather. She didn't want to leave Pa there, all by himself. The paradox of the situation confused her and had led her nowhere when she saw smoke rising from the village. Her biggest fear was that they had set fire to the granaries in the houses, since that was what her mother and aunt had been most concerned about. But the child that she was, she found more comfort in staying close to her dead father's corpse than going home.

After a few hours, the sun had risen to add a tingly sense of warmth to the dusty morning and was glowering with its full might. Farida had cried beside her dead father so much that her eyes were dry and she could not weep any more. She was still half hidden in the wheat field with her father's blood clotting on the soil which he had cultivated all his life. Her heart ached for her family. She was sure the people must have hidden somewhere when their houses were being set on fire. It didn't break her heart as much as the loss of her father did, since they were already taking the train to Lahore. They could just stay there. How different could it be? After all, Patiala and Lahore were both cities of the same Punjab.

It must have been around noon when the swarm of angry-looking men, armed with spears, daggers and lit torches left the premise of the village which had been reduced to ashes. Farida realized her father had to be buried, and for that, the family had to be told. As she neared the village, the stench of ashes and burnt leather became stronger and denser. Even at the threshold of the village where she stood, near the huge oak tree that provided shelter to the village elders every morning and evening, the smell was unbearable. The oak was still on fire. Behind it, the mud structures had been reduced to blocks of charcoal. She was bewildered and ran towards her house. As she raced past the other houses, she could hear moans from a few, but was too caught up with fear for her own family. Her legs, small and trembling, took her to the locked door of her house. She unbolted the door to see her grandfather lying face down in the courtyard, blood trickling from his belly. In her haste, she unbolted the room and as the creaky wooden planks swung open, a huge cloud of smoke hit her face. It smelled like burnt leather. It was dark inside. The walls, the floor and the ceiling were all black, so she had to try harder to make out what was happening. She spotted some stiff rolls in black, but could not understand what they were.

As she went closer, she realized that they were, in fact, human bodies.

Her family had turned to coal. Tears gushed once again from her eyes, which had almost dried from weeping over her father. She wailed in a hoarse voice, walking through the room, trying hard to differentiate the wooden blocks that had been the charpoys, from dead bodies. Her two breast-fed brothers had become rigid in her mother's arms. Her howls grew louder and she sat on the ground.

She suddenly felt a hand on her bald head. Startled, she looked up to see her Abbaji's face. He had spread one of his arms across his chest to stop the blood from flowing. With the other, he picked Farida up, and as she clung to his neck, he made light shushing sounds. He warned her, saying, 'Don't make a noise,

## Farida

they will hear us…shush, shush… Now tell me where is Pa?' He had to repeat himself a few times before she could tell him that he was dead. He didn't say anything.

Abbaji, the wise old man that he was, had done well when his family was ambushed. He had bravely secured the women, children and his younger son in the room, which nonetheless, had been sprayed with kerosene and set fire to, by the attackers. They had first confronted Laal, who fell on the ground after taking one blow from a sword, and did what a mouse does when the cat gets too close—play dead. They had left him lying there, and thus, he escaped the fire. He had gathered his courage when he heard Farida's voice and had walked up to the sole heir of his family.

As soon as he had picked her up, she rested her head on his shoulder. She did not go to sleep, but the shock had gotten to her head and her senses had become numb. She felt her Abbaji taking off her flower-printed shirt and pulling her cousin Jamal's shirt over her head. Her loyal, white lattha salwar and the blue kurta made her look like a bald-headed boy. He lifted her up again. He had not forgotten the time of the train, and hiding through bushes and burnt crops, smuggled himself and Farida to the train station.

The station was lined up with sentry officers. Most of them were Hindus and Sikhs. They had started to feel secure, for the officers-on-duty helped the bewildered lot. Many people boarded the train and all the passengers had one thing in common—the befuddlement on their faces. A girl of Farida's age sat beside them, with her mother. She stared at Farida, who also stared back.

Farida closed her eyes when she could look no more. She kept hearing the girl's voice; she was asking her mother, 'Where are we going, Ammi?'

Her mother answered, 'Lahore.'

'When we last went to Lahore to the house of Dada's brother, we took mithai for them. Did you forget the mithai, Ammi? Also, will you take me to the Badshahi Masjid this time, too?'

The mother was as still as a statue. She was stunned and didn't reply. When Laal and Farida—heartbroken and deserted—finally stepped down from the train at Lahore, the red dust reminded her of the field where her father had died, the humid air was reminiscent of the upcoming monsoon back home, and the strange faces around them were a constant reminder that lives had been ruined on both sides of the border.

Laal had sustained a deep wound. His chest was diagonally cut, but the vest he wore under his shirt was lined with currency notes stitched on the inside. His savings had been the shield of his soft, wrinkly flesh. He told Farida during the train ride that he had fallen to the ground, shut his eyes and held his breath, until the carnage had subsided. She asked him if he, too, had had to fight off the urge to help the family like she had. He smiled painfully and shook his head.

The refugee camp, where both of them had to stay for several months, was unhygienic and they both had to take turns every day to clean the pus from Abbaji's wounds. However, sometime later, the government found a hole-like house for them in the remnants of the walled city set up by the Mughals within Lahore.

*Farida*

Farida and her Abbaji lived in the barren womb of this metropolis. The innards of Lahore bled with wounded men. It howled with the shrieks of raped women. It blistered with the wails of orphaned children. And it stayed like this for a few decades. Everyone had the same story to tell, everyone was awaiting a family member to appear out of nowhere. Sometimes they did. A young woman came back to her father seven months after the partition. She was pregnant; her belly as swollen as the sacks of wheat from Farida's father's granary. She had wrapped her bulbous body around her father, amid tears of relief. Women stuffed the edges of their scarves in their mouths and men turned up their noses in disgust. However, the father had pushed his daughter and walked away, annoying Farida. The next morning, the neighbours pulled up a young woman's lifeless body from the local well. Farida sneaked her face in between the portly buttocks of two other ladies to see who it was.

It was the same girl who had returned to her father the previous day.

In a matter of months, they ran out of the money Laal had brought with him. They had to feed themselves since the rations at the refugee camp would not suffice their weekly needs. Laal, the skeletal old man, carried sacks of whatever load the supervisor at the construction site asked him to transport—cement, sand, gravel or rocks. Farida witnessed him make bricks at the kiln, while she sat in the shade with torn and battered books the schoolmaster gave away as charity to pupils like her.

She had tried to study but the conditions weren't favourable. Old man Laal got sick every other day and Farida had to spoon-feed him like a baby. The winters had been frightening. Other than Jamal's blue kurta and the lattha salwar, she had been bestowed with a sweater and a ratty blanket by the social workers. Laal had been a proud man for the early weeks of winter when he blatantly refused hand-me-downs. Later, when the fog became thick and cloudy, and wrapped them while they slept in camp beds in the bare house they had been allotted, Laal had to finally swallow his pride. He accepted a worn-out tweed jacket.

But it was too late. He was struck down with pneumonia, coughing all day and spitting blood at night. Refugees, who had grown a liking to this odd pair of a helpful old man and cute little girl, came over to enquire after him. One of those men was a young schoolmaster. He was thin, frail, bespectacled, and wore a very stern expression on his face. All three months of winter that Farida's grandfather was sick, he visited them every week. Sometimes, he brought them something to eat—a handful of palm sugar or a couple of apples. Even for the farmers, who had churned sugar out of cane juice and stored them in enormous canisters back home, the handful was no less than a luxury.

After nine months of their arrival in Lahore, Farida hit puberty. She didn't even know what was happening to her. She told her grandfather and he suddenly looked older. He started to weep silently. Farida thought she must be dying and asked him if that was the case. He looked at her sadly and said, 'I am the one dying, bitiya.'

Laal did the best he could to secure her future, and gave her away as a child-bride to the schoolmaster, who already had a wife and a child. Those were the days of looting and ransacking.

## Farida

Although the partition began and ended the same day, the raiding and raping continued. The safest option for her, after her grandfather, was with the schoolmaster, also called Master Saab. Or that is what she was told by Abbaji. Even if she had doubts about that, they were all eased after a month of her nikah, when Laal passed away and she was the wife of an educated, salaried man. The nikah was done at the closest masjid. Farida was exceptionally happy because, after an entire year, she had received a new pair of clothes—red and gold-coloured. 'Oh, how pretty you look!' Master Saab had said when his first wife left them alone in the room later that night.

The first thing Laal had said to Farida in Lahore, was, 'Remember Farida, violence always begets violence, hate always begets hate.' Later in life, she learnt many phrases, idioms and moral lessons which reminded her of her grandfather's words. Those words answered all the questions that she had had about her Pa even without asking anyone, and she wished, till her last breath, that he hadn't gone out that night.

# Reema
*The keeper of secrets*

$\mathscr{A}$ very miniscule number of people would ever have the courage to say that their childhood wasn't a bed of roses. Interpersonal information apart, one can read books filled with memoirs, cherish poetry oozing with nostalgia and watch films that focus on the innocence affiliated with the time span when heads are filled with restless inquisitiveness, devilish naughtiness and constant curiosity.

For someone who has seen childhood, parenthood and even grandparenthood, it can be firmly said that out of all these, childhood is the one that a person sweetly reminisces about. However, the same cannot be said about Reema, who had, for years, mentally stayed in that period of time when she was ten. You see, she has Alzheimer's.

It had been two years since her stay at the hospice. This was the second day during all this time that she had been able to distinguish between the past and the present. She didn't exactly know when it happened the last time, but she could recall that the feeling was strange. It was like waking up from a deep sleep, an enticing dream that one wants to keep dreaming, the one that keeps whispering in the ear, 'Sleep a little more…just a little… finish the dream…'

When one wakes up from such dreams, usually a healthy, youthful brain takes a couple of seconds to separate the imaginary from the real. And when it's a crippled brain like Reema's, it is a herculean task to bring one's mind back in touch with reality, in the room of a hospice sans companionship. When in a trance, she had been surrounded by her family and friends—Mom, Dad, her younger brother Waqas, her best friend Laila, and most of the time, her favourite, Uncle Billu.

Billu was her father's younger brother. He was ten years younger than her father, so that made him fourteen when she was born. Her grandparents were farmers—simpletons who had made a life out of rearing livestock and farming vegetables. Reema's father, Aslam, had been the nerd who won his school and college seats through scholarships and some aid from the Young Christian Men's Association. An apprenticeship during law school had helped Aslam settle out of the muddy land where his parents lived, into the metropolis of Karachi. Both her parents had often mentioned how hard it was to find a house or apartment in the city. It is always overflowing with jobseekers and every cheap and not-so-cheap abode is, most of the time, already taken. Aslam had managed to secure a small three-bedroom apartment in the dingy area of Nazimabad. The tiny ground floor was all he could offer to his wife when he proposed to her for marriage. Reema's mother, Nargis, being a secretary to Aslam's boss, had often told her daughter how she fell in love with Aslam's slight stammer when he spoke to her. His nervousness, his fidgeting fingers and restless eyes made her want to hug him so tight that all the awkwardness between them would vanish.

'How did he propose to you?'

At ten, it was getting pretty confusing for Reema to imagine how her father could have asked for her mother's hand in marriage. He still had a stutter in his voice. Nargis told her he did a fine job, but Reema secretly thought it must have been her mother who had put forth the question in the end.

Her mother loved talking about their courtship in the office, when her father, as a clerk, could not afford lavish five-star dinners but only a Friday night movie starring Amitabh Bachchan (her mother's favourite) with a desi burger and cold drink for dinner from the stall outside the cinema. She loved talking about her wedding day, when all dressed-up, she was waiting in her chamber at the church and Aslam was twenty minutes late. She had sweated away her makeup, thinking her stuttering fiancé had gotten cold feet and stood her up.

'You won't believe what he looked like!' Nargis would sway from side to side telling the story. Her laughter was like that… it bubbled out of her. Her sadness was also the same… it oozed out of her. Reema could fairly imagine what she must have gone through during those twenty minutes.

'He came in looking like a homeless man, his jacket open

and flapping on both sides, his bowtie undone and hanging from his neck, and his shoes, dusty as a camel's fur. He had been to the train station to receive his parents and had been caught up in a traffic jam. While your paternal grandparents' rickshaw arrived at the venue just before we were serving mithai to the guests after a simple dinner of chicken biryani, chicken qorma and zarda, your father had raced all the way down to the church, just to be in time.'

Reema noticed her mother savoured every detail of the story each time she told it. She loved the story, too. Sometimes Uncle Billu would be there, as her mother poured out the wedding tale. He would also punctuate her monologue with his snorts, chuckles and laughter.

'Yeah, and I was the best man, chhoti.' He would ruffle Reema's hair while addressing her with the nickname he had given her, and was used exclusively by him. Billu, her mother used to say, was her first child. He was fourteen when her mother got married, and since it was impossible for her father to pull his stubborn parents out of their countryside farm, he had made an effort to get Billu enrolled into a public school in Karachi.

'He can d-d-d-do better, better than m-m-m-e,' Aslam used to say.

And so, Billu had been a part of their household even before Reema had arrived into this world. He was like an older brother to Reema and also like a young uncle. Most of her early childhood memories were with him. He played many games such as catch and chased butterflies with her. She often narrated the stories to her children and grandchildren.

What ailed her, though, is what she didn't tell anyone.

Despite her disease, she had trouble talking about the events that had changed her life forever. However, she had nothing left to lose, and she thought of her posterity—her granddaughters—who were then exactly the same age as she was when she had experienced one of the harshest truths about human nature. It's weird how much time had passed since then, when she was ten, and now, when she was eighty, lying in seclusion in a hospice bed, awaiting her last breath. Most of her life during the past two years had been spent in delusion—she had been reliving her childhood and all those days that she spent with her beloved Uncle Billu. It was painful but she decided that she shall not delay this any more, for it could be the last time she woke up into reality. Who knew, she might never be able to tell the tale of Billu. The forceful rush of memories was gushing through her brain and she deemed it fit to pour out the reminiscence once and for all, before the tide of forgetfulness washed over and took her back to the tranquil world of oblivion.

⁓

Summer in Reema's childhood home was always the season she looked forward to. Most kids do, because they get off from school. But for Reema, the reason used to be different—she used to wait for the school session to end so she could get to see Uncle Billu, who was a boarder at his school. He used to come around for Easter, Eid, Christmas and the summer holidays. Probably the best thing about being a Christian in Pakistan is that you would get double Eidee and double holidays.

## Reema

She always yearned for Billu's visit, awaited his presents and even if his presents were nothing she needed, she would keep them safe, locked away in her treasure chest, which was hidden under the stack of dolls next to her nightstand.

For her tenth birthday that year, he got her a fake ivory inkpot and quill. She had no idea what to do with it until he told her what it meant to have the quill.

'In the olden days,' Billu said (he was a gifted storyteller), 'when people used nothing but bits of charcoal and raw lead to write or make signs, there lived a young man who had a pet phoenix. Now phoenixes are supposed to be very bad-tempered birds. They screech when agitated and, sometimes, if the narrator wants to put an overly-dramatic effect to the story, they can even breathe fire.'

Billu held the quill firmly in his hands (as if it had the power to grow wings and fly away, if given the chance) as he sat on the sofa next to the TV set. Reema sat on the shaggy rug her mother would, each year, religiously spread near the TV, exclusively for Christmas. She didn't know what she looked like with her big black eyes agape and her cherry red mouth pouted in anticipation of what universal secrets Billu was about to spill in the form of the story about the quill. What she did know is that Billu stared at her for the longest time. At ten, she was getting curious by the microsecond, about what the quill meant, and he seemed in no hurry to complete his tale.

'The young man had no friends, so his pet phoenix was his only companion. He used to write stories—you read stories?'

He kept her involved in the tale and dragged it a little, like a frustratingly mysterious act. One kept longing for the words to come out of his mouth so that the curiosity could be soothed; he kept one enthralled. She nodded fiercely when he asked her about reading stories.

'Well, he kept his phoenix by his side all day when he wrote, and even at night, when the lamp on his dresser didn't have enough oil to burn a flame bright enough for him to keep writing. It didn't bother him—the darkness—for he was young, and my dear Reema, when a man is young, he does not care much about such things.'

Billu stopped to stretch.

'So, what did he care about?' she asked him.

Billu stared at her briefly and said, 'He wanted a companion, you know! Someone to stroke his hand and someone to run her fingers through his hair.'

'Mommy does that to me when I am not sleepy,' she said in an all-knowing tone.

Billu smiled as he looked at her. 'You are the most innocent creature ever, my darling.'

He ran a finger across her cheek.

'So, what happened next?'

'Well, one day he was writing vigorously, for he had to tie up a tale for some money, when his pen broke. You know the nib of a pen is fragile and too much pressure can crack it. So, it happened, and he was devastated. He mourned the loss of his only pen, when the phoenix perched on the headrest of his bed, flew over to the table and handed him a quill. The man didn't know at first what to do with it until the phoenix pecked him on the hand with its pointed beak. He howled a little since the peck caused some blood to ooze from his skin, and the phoenix, firmly holding the quill in its beak, dipped the pointed end of the quill into the blood and drew a line on the table.'

'It didn't take him long to say "eureka" and it was before the sun rose that he had finished his story.'

Billu was staring at the quill when she asked him, 'What was he writing about?'

He pondered for a second. 'Stuff...' he shrugged, adding, 'Grown-up stuff.'

'Did it have a happy ending?'

'I hope so.' He smiled.

'Reema! Billu! Come over, kids!'

It was her mother calling out for dinner after the table was set.

They were simple people. A set table for Christmas meant a roast chicken, pulao and fruit trifle. There were additional condiments, too—laughter and love.

Reema later felt that when her own children had taken her to their homes for a Christmas dinner, there was too much fancy stuff around, and on the table. There were things that she had never heard of, such as tinsels and scented candles and bottled sauces and designer wear. Christmas must be celebrated like before, she thought. Reema missed the age when she could proudly strut her way down to the church, hold mass, sing hymns and do the lot. People could dress up in their finest and the newspapers printed special editions to wish 'Happy Christmas' to all the Christian brethren in Pakistan and elsewhere. Her favourite memory, however, was the way the bakeries and churches were lit up as if they were celebrating Eid or Independence Day. The sense of belonging she got was so uplifting. She had seen her children having a hard time being Christians in Pakistan. The extremists didn't think twice before burning down an entire neighbourhood of Christians or slapping the law of blasphemy on anyone. One had to be very careful.

Anyhow, they had the poshest dinner they had ever had—a whole roasted lamb and vegetable biryani. While she had been busy using her meat-shredding skills on the lamb's butt that her mother had carved for her, the parents were busy talking to Billu. They were asking a lot of questions. She remembered the words, which were trapped somewhere in the swirl of her vocabulary but she wouldn't be able to repeat them now if asked to.

Nargis was asking him about how he planned to get a job after his college was over next year. She also asked him to find a good girl.

'A man cannot be balanced without a woman,' she had said.

When Billu said he didn't quite get the remark, Aslam started a long, boring talk about two tightrope walkers, one man and the other, a woman, and how they balance each other. Billu said he wasn't ready to settle down.

Aslam rose from the table, his face dark and grim. His voice boomed above Reema's head and the whole room seemed to fill with it. He was yelling about the gang Billu had at college and that they were going to get him into trouble.

'The day you get arrested for doing dope and hooch with those bastards, don't you dare take my name for bail this time.'

## Reema

Aslam had slammed his glass of homemade wine on the table and it smashed into a hundred pieces. Nargis came over and held him from behind, hugging him and begging him to calm down, for Billu was 'just a boy'. Billu had stormed out of the room and had disappeared into the darkness. All the while, Reema sat, gaping at them all, her mouth stuffed with unchewed lamb and rice.

After dinner, it was Dad's turn to tuck her in bed. She had the quill under her pillow as she slept. She was scared to ask Dad for a bedtime story so she just kissed him back when he told her that she was his little princess. She was thinking whether Uncle Billu had come back or not and it worried her. She was happy thinking the phoenix was going to stay with her forever through its feather. What made it more special was that Billu had given it to her for her tenth Christmas.

The best thing about Christmas was that it came with lots of holidays. To Reema, that meant lots of time with Billu. Even Laila, her best friend, who lived just a lane away, would come over and the two of them would play cricket, teatime or board games with Billu. During those holidays, when she had felt so important for owning a quill, her mother had to suddenly go visit Reema's sick grandmother.

'I shall be gone three days,' she whispered into Reema's ear, while holding her tight.

'Who shall fix my breakie?' She tried to pout and sound like a baby, but her mother had everything planned and under her belt.

'Sweetie, Daddy will give you breakfast and dinner. Billu shall be here all three days, and if you get hungry, he can get you your favourite shami kabab sandwich for lunch or Mommy's aloo tikki from the freezer. Okay?'

She was happy to have Uncle Billu all to herself for three days. The games she could play with him were limitless and the happiness in her heart was beyond her. Mothers are very perceptive of their children. The fun part is, the kids think they are opaque, but in fact, they are as transparent as sheer silk, and mothers can see right through them.

'I will miss you,' she purred and her mother smiled.

'No, you won't.' She kissed her forehead, picked up her bag and hugged her a little before walking through the door. Reema gagged silently when her father held her in his arms for a long, quiet kiss, after which she ran into her room, getting her board games in order to use them when Billu woke up.

Billu always had his own room in their house. Nargis had plans to change it into a nursery if she was going to have another baby, but that wouldn't happen until the next year. After setting up the carom board, and the monopoly game aunt Azra had given to her for her birthday, Reema had tidied up her dolls, brushing and braiding their hair and straightening their skirts until she could spruce them up no more. The wait for Billu was trying. Reema's father popped in his head to say goodbye, for the lawyer's office would not wait for him any longer. She ran to kiss him on the cheek and whispered in his ear to bring her some cotton candy on his way back home. Her father smiled and put out his pinkie. She wrapped hers with his. This was going to be the best vacation ever. Now only if Uncle Billu would wake up.

After a while, Reema couldn't wait any more so she decided

to take things into her own hands. She tiptoed from her room to his, opened the door as silently as a mouse would, crept inside and saw him snoring. He was looking and sounding funny. The snores were sounding like the ice-cream truck's engine when it halts at the street's end. She muffled her giggles with both hands. A streak of drool was trickling out of his mouth and running down his cheek. She went closer to see where the drool went and saw a wet patch on his pillow. Yuck! She thought of all the times her mother tucked this 'extra' pillow under her head when she was lying on the sofa, watching *Mickey Mouse*. It was disgusting!

She rubbed her sleeve against her cheek, trying to wipe off whatever residue that pillow must have left on her skin, and tried to take some revenge. She stepped backwards, aimed to perfection (she had practiced this on her father every Sunday), ran the two metres between the door and the bed, and jumped right over Billu who was sleeping under the sheets.

'Whaaaaa?' He woke up from his dream, startled, puzzled and aghast.

Reema went nuts punching him with her tiny fists, laughing and enjoying the moment. When Billu came to comprehend what was happening, he also played along, tickling her in response to her punching and trying to lay her off until she screamed with laughter, 'Stop, stop!'

Decades later, her grandchildren also found out about this soft spot, and two of them, Sobia and Beenish, Reema's daughter's daughters, tickled her feet when the rocking chair had lulled her to sleep. Naughty brats, she would chuckle.

## Unfettered Wings

Age is just a number, they say. That is only partially true, though. Age is a complete measuring unit of human capacity and ability. Babies, born anywhere in the world, have similar needs. A toddler is vigorously going through a learning phase as a young body has its needs and desires. Old age, well, has its curses. Reema's curse had been Alzheimer's. It's a pity, really, that more than the suffering from the ailment, she was afraid of its reoccurrence. It was like a phobia. She was afraid of her disease when it was not there, and her senses were completely engulfed by it when it consumed her being. Thus, it became more than Alzheimer's. It became like a physical threat that overshadowed every nook and corner of her walking trail. She felt as if she would never be prepared for the moment when it would jump out of nowhere and devour her in its dark shroud of nothingness.

When she was ten, her bogeyman used to be imaginary—a monster under the bed or a spider in the closet. But the day Nargis left her alone with Billu, her bogeyman changed. The innocent, ten-year old that she was, became a person who she couldn't relate to any more. And it all started as soon as Billu stopped tickling her on his bed.

Breathless as they both were, she was lying still on her uncle's torso. 'I want to play with you,' she told him.

'Yeah?' he groaned a little.

She didn't hear the wryness in his voice then, but the conversation has lingered on her cognitive mind for so long, that later, she could dissect it like a surgeon who apart different layers of the skin and puts them back accurately.

Billu, however, wasn't very happy at the prospect of leaving his bed and playing cards with her.

'Yes! Mommy is at Grammy's for three days and Daddy is at office. We have the house to ourselves and we are going to play and play and play!' Her voice was shrill and quivering with excitement. She had sat up on his legs and her arms flailed around her as she spoke of the freedom.

Billu had a weird expression on his face. She had never seen his face as dark as that. There was a sheen in his eyes; a glisten that she couldn't recognize. As she awaited a response from him, he moved his hands under the sheets.

'Hey, Chhoti, guess what?'

She beamed her biggest smile. 'What?'

'I got a new game for you,' he said, grinning.

'Yay!' She jumped down from the bed, anticipating a sport of sorts.

'No, come back! We have to play here on the bed.' He gestured her to come sit near his legs.

She obeyed like a dog. He was like that to her, the human she could love and trust with her eyes closed and senses shut down.

'Okay Chhoti, I have a bar of chocolate hidden somewhere under the sheets and I need you to find it. But you can't peep underneath, okay? No cheating at all.' He almost glared towards the end of his instructions.

'If I can't see, then how will I find it?' She was confused.

'Feel for it, with your hands.'

It had been seventy years—seven decades, three quarters of a century—since this painful episode of her life, and yet she could not talk about it without feeling that it had been her fault...that she should have tried to stop him...that she was not that much of a dunce...but then, maybe she was. She had been cooking up the best defence for years, and the best she had done was, 'I was stupid.'

From that age when she remembered nothing much, Billu's smirk got imprinted on her mind in such a way that she could even see it in her husband's smile when they shared moments of intimacy. She would lie there, dreading that the sanctity and purity of the romance would be tarnished by a similar grin that had wrecked her notions of familiarity, trust and unconditional love.

That day Billu raped her. It was after a long time that she fully realized what had happened during a game of blind man's buff, up in the attic. All she knew was that she had a blindfold and was laughing, trying to grab Billu as he made whistling sounds from here and there, and suddenly, something strong pinned her against the wall from behind so fiercely that her cheek got bruised against the rough paint. She was standing with her face and hands crushed against the wall. What hurt most was the pain—the excruciating pain that was the worst—and it made her cringe for years after. She screamed for Billu to help her. She screamed that something was hurting her, but he never came around for help. Later, when she was lying like a rag doll on the attic floor, she had to muster up energy to untie the blindfold and found blood on her pants and the floor.

When Aslam came home that evening, Billu still hadn't returned. Reema was in her room, huddled on her bed, trying not to move or expose an inch of her being outside the blanket.

## Reema

She had been crying; anyone could stand a kilometre away and know that she had been doling out tears by the bucket. Her father called out her name when he entered the house but she was too feeble to reply. He called out for Billu, but he had vanished while she was being manhandled by an invisible force. When her father came to her room, the colour drained from his face and he kept asking what was wrong and where Billu was, but all she could say was, 'I want Mommy.' By the end of the night, she was at her grandmother's.

She told her mother that she had fallen down in the attic and had her face bruised. Nargis felt her all over but she was unhurt except for blue and black fingerprints around her arms. She asked Reema what those were and she didn't know what to say. She hurriedly dressed Reema in a shirt, and turned to leave the room. Reema could hear her mother sob from a distance. They never talked about those bruises after that night.

Billu was never seen again. Once Reema asked her mother if they had reported about him to the police and she never gave an answer. Reema had formed a theory in her ten-year-old brain—extra-terrestrial beings had hurt her and taken Billu away. Oh, how she wished it was true! She could have lived better with the pain of losing her Uncle Billu to a bunch of aliens than having to live with the pain of being a victim to his lechery.

It took her years to fully understand why her father had lectured Billu to get a woman. He must have seen the spark in his brother's eyes—the spark that makes a human appear beastly; the despicable, agitated and rapacious look that one man can recognize in another, especially around his own women. She also realized later in life what her mother must have understood immediately. Her observant eyes did not need a second proof to know what caused bruises on her daughter's arms and why she had bled in the toilet for a day or two afterwards. She silently slid a hot water bottle under Reema's bottom as she put her to bed each night. No questions asked, no reasons given. Reema saw many changes in her mother after that night and one was the absence of her bubbly laughter. She laughed at jokes, sure; she was a lively person. But she stopped swaying with her cackles.

Her mother became very protective of Reema's whereabouts, too. To Reema, it was as if her motherly instincts had gone crazy. She accompanied her everywhere until Reema got sick of it and protested. Reema didn't quite realize why Uncle Billu had disappeared. She only noticed that her parents had stopped talking about him.

The first thing Nargis did when they came home from her grandmother's house was to turn Billu's bedroom into a sewing room. Reema asked her meekly where Billu would sleep when he came home. She didn't reply for several moments and Reema saw her lips purse tightly, as if she was trying hard to stop the words escaping her mouth. When she finally looked at her daughter, she searched the small, innocent face, held both her daughter's arms in her hands and said softly, 'Billu won't come here, Reema. He has gone to a faraway place.'

Her eyes were fierce as she spoke, but her tone was as soft as silk. Well, it was only three years later that Waqas, Reema's baby brother, arrived and her mother shoved the sewing machine back into the kitchen to turn Billu's room into a nursery. They never spoke of him after that.

∽

It must be said that Billu disappeared that day and did not turn up until Nargis died, twelve years later. Reema would have been devastated if not for Peter. It was an emotionally distressful time for her. Both because she had her mother lying in a coffin in front of her and also because Billu had shown face after all these years. He looked at her from the corner of the room, while they mourned her dead mother. Reema was twenty-two and her fiancé Peter was with her. He dared not come closer or speak to his victim. She did have to admit to herself, though, that as soon as their eyes met, she clung fiercely to Peter, not because she was scared, but because she had a need to show him off. Peter tried to loosen her grip on his arm, but he stopped after looking into her imploring eyes.

A slight guilt of hers was never having told Peter that she had felt tainted even before she knew the meaning of the word. It's not that he wouldn't have understood. He would have been her rock, if she had let him. He would even have made sure she never saw Billu again, which she didn't. But she always expected to spot him in every new place she went to. Every dinner, wedding or hike she went on, was not without the fear of seeing him— her bogeyman—leap out of nowhere and stand in front of her, hidden behind white sheets, looking at her with those eyes and that satisfied smile on his face that had damaged her for good.

∽

'Forever' was a funny word to Reema, especially now that she had almost reached her 'forever.' She had seen her parents die, her brother pass away, her children grow up and her grandchildren bloom into young adults. She had felt loved by Peter, who, she could still witness, visited her every Sunday as per the visitor chart hanging on her door knob. She didn't remember when she last saw him, though.

'Poor guy,' she thought to herself, 'he must put up with my disease every time, and come back again. I owe him… I owe him an apology for not making him part of my pain then, while he so dedicatedly is a part of my pain now.

She spoke into the air, as the momentum drew closer and Alzheimer's was ready to pounce on her memory with full force.

'Peter, this is the bit of me that I held back from you. This is the part of my soul that I didn't bare to you. This is why I never hired a babysitter and you had to go through droughts of wifely attention when the babies held all of mine.'

'I owe an apology to myself for not opening up about Billu to my parents or Peter. I pushed myself into isolation and social boycott. I spent a lonely, colourless teenage and I shunned all friendships. I was paranoid, regressive and moody. I needed help. I refused to get it. I was the victim but I was made to feel as if I was the wrongdoer.'

The only person who could penetrate that thick skin of hers and reach for her heart was Peter, her husband and former boss at the call centre he owned. His genteel behaviour and kind eyes, his debonair manners and soft-spoken tone assured her

## Reema

that he was nothing like Billu. He had to wait for a year before she let him into her heart.

'I have loved you Peter, for reasons I never disclosed and more than I ever said.

'I hope and pray that we have taught our daughters and daughters-in-law to secure their relationships with their spouses and their children. Tell them; for I am getting tired and drowsy, and when I wake up later—if I do—I won't be able to tell you any of this. Thank you for putting up with me when I am not in my right mind. When it's time, bury me with my wedding ring. I had had this in mind when I ended my vows with "yours, forever".'

She wanted to say more. She wanted to apologize to her mother for being the pain of her heart. She wanted to say that as her daughter, she should have talked about what happened. Maybe they could have gone to therapy together. Nargis didn't have to take the burden of her daughter's rape on her soul alone. Maybe she tried to deal with the damage to Reema's personality just like she dealt with the heartbreak Billu gave her. Nargis probably felt that she had failed with both because she tried to do everything alone. Reema had wanted to say all this and a lot more to her mother, but unfortunately, wasn't able to.

As dusk was approaching, the small window in her room showed her a patch of green outside, where some people like her were taking a stroll. Some were crippled and had nurses behind them to push their wheelchairs. Karachi had advanced from what she remembered it to be. She silently wished that her children and grandchildren would experience more ease living here than she ever had.

She felt sleepy. Soon, the nurse would be there to give her some pills and after those, she would again drift off to sheer emptiness. Faces of her beloved children and grandchildren were flickering like candlelights across her eyes. She, after such a tiring mental exercise of rummaging through the empty caskets of a Christmas past, made an effort to keep her eyes open, for once she would enter the chasm of sleep, who knows from which point the spool of memories would start to unwind.

Despite the creeping fear and the knowledge of going into the realm of her past, she felt weightless. She had said it decades later, when she should have said it earlier and probably made another girl safe from Billu. She did learn later that he had gotten convicted for a co-worker's rape twenty years ago. Brave girl, that one. She did what Reema thought she should have done… decades ago.

As the nurse pulled her wheelchair away from the window, Reema was frantically saying:

'I feel terrible. I want my Mommy. I need to talk to her. I need to tell her all this.

'Mommy? Can I come to Grammy's with you? Please?'

# Maria
### *The wanton one*

*H*ave you ever run your fingers through the velveteen fabric of an abrisham Persian rug? If you have, then you know what it means when it is said that the Persian rug, made with the most delicate of natural silk threads, is more than a composition of knotted fibres—it is a story spun over months, maybe years. If you have never had the chance to caress abrisham, then you need to hear this tale. But before that, I must tell you what is abrisham.

'Abrisham' is Persian for silk. Mind you, there are many kinds of Persian rugs, but abrisham is the most opulent of them all. While buyers of an abrisham rug might be more interested in the intricate details of the pattern a craftsman has woven, the tiny errors that escape an ordinary eye are of a greater interest to a skilled merchant who knows the flaws made by a weaver. The merchant might not disclose the flaws, but in his heart, he always knows the worth and value of each piece in his possession. The merchant notices it all—the sudden indent of a misplaced thread in a pattern, the lack of a lustrous white fibre which could have added gleam to the sword of the swordsman in the design, and the spare thread, clumsily torn, that has left a miniscule trace of a different colour at the hem of the rug.

This tale, too, is about such a merchant who began the early days of his business during desperate times. But before you get into that, you need to know about the boredom of his early days, when he couldn't take any more of the desert life in Kharan, Balochistan, in south-western Pakistan. The heat and expanse of sand is what he had grown up with, but it was the lack of colourful objects in that desert which pained his heart. Sometimes, he imagined swaying, lush trees. He also imagined the poplar tree—sturdy, sprawling and with a thick trunk. The backdrop in the mental images was always a sky the colour of heather. The trees provided shade to a red divan. There, among the cushions on the couch, he imagined a woman. She was faceless but she was perfect. He imagined further and deeper, until the painful throb in his heart would become unbearable.

The images helped for a while to escape the daft reality of his surroundings, but then came a time when they didn't work for him any more. His environs echoed with poetry being sung to the rhythm of the dutar; yet, he yearned to get out of them.

Have you ever heard of a dutar? If you haven't had the experience of listening to the symphony of the mystical, two-stringed instrument of the desert, you will not understand the psyche of the protagonist. The simple-looking musical apparatus, with two cords wound across a long-necked wooden vessel, produces a sound that may not be considered for a grand orchestra of sorts, but is so titillating that the vibrations reach from the eardrum to a place deep inside, connecting the nerve cells of the entire human body. The music is so high-pitched that it keeps ringing in the listeners' ears for a long time after the dutar had stopped playing. It becomes really haunting at times.

Sometimes the men from the protagonist Baseer's tribe, tired after a day of labour, sat around a small bonfire at night, a kettle of traditional qehwa (a type of green tea made without milk or sugar) boiling atop the fire. One of them would grab a dutar and sing a lover's ballad or mourn a lost love. The music would possess Baseer, though he would try to walk away at times. But the tingling sensation the pitch of the dutar would create right at his ear lobes, would crawl like a menace under his skin and become an unscratchable itch, reminding him of places he couldn't reach.

Now, like any young man wouldn't, and couldn't, take any more, he decided to flee. He tried to get away from it all, but the ties pulled him down—the family, the shop assistant's job he did to contribute to his parents' income, and also the guilt that came out of explaining why he needed to leave.

'I want to make a better living,' he announced. His mother didn't want him to go, and neither did his father. But even though the plan he had was not altogether a risky one, the questions his family asked were unending.

'How will you live out there?'
'When will you come back?'

'How would we know you are well?'

'What will you do?'

He let all of them have their say and replied with one word—carpets.

So, carpets were to become his way of life. He first took a train from Kharan, and then a bus to Zahedan, a city in Sistan, Iran. He marvelled at the similarity of culture, race and geography between the two deserts on the two sides of the Durand Line. In Zahedan, half the population spoke Farsi and the other half spoke Balochi. Baseer could converse in both. The bus had dropped him off at Rassouli Bazaar, which was a long lane full of goodies on either side. The passers-by and shoppers made for one big mixed mob.

Baseer stood still where the bus had unloaded the passengers, letting his eyes take it all in. He thrust his hand in the pocket of his shirt to assure himself that the small amount of money he had borrowed from his uncles and father as a capital to start his business, was securely tucked in. It was.

He walked around shops of copper and bronze jewellery, tikkas and kebabs, as well as naan tandoors and cloth, until he arrived at a shop which sold what he had come to buy.

The small, cabin-like shop was lined with rugs of the most intricate patterns known to the human eye. The most common pattern was that of a vase with blooming flowers. The vase was of the same form on all those rugs, which carried it as some sort of an emblem; however, the colours separated them all. If the background was royal blue, the flowers spurting forth would be pink, ochre and cyan. Against a grey background, the flowers were a more calming sky blue, magenta and olive. It was setting his senses on fire. He asked for the price of one, and after haggling for a while, he had three of these magnificent rugs rolled up, tied with a thin rope and all ready to be bundled onto his back.

'Where to, young man?' the shopkeeper asked in Farsi.

'Lahore,' he replied, grinning ear to ear. Half of his dream was fulfilled and he was determined to fulfil the other half in what what also known as the City of Gardens.

The details of his voyage to Lahore, or how he found a place to sleep, are unnecessary. Let's just say his only possessions were the three exquisite-looking rugs he carried on his back, and a few rupees in his pockets that bought him a meal per day. He initially loitered around the train station, but the poor desert fellow soon found himself a little lost. He would gape at the tall buildings, with four or five floors in a single structure.

There is nothing of grandeur in some localities of Lahore. But Baseer was not a settler. He had come to roam the city. His wanderings took him from the station to the walled city, an area that took pride in being the remains of the Mughal Raj. There, he saw ancient buildings and houses that, despite the moss-covered walls, wore a majestic look. He walked through the dingy lanes of Heera Mandi, a red-light neighbourhood popular for its courtesans. Legend has it that the army of Mughal emperors always took a day or two of rest here, when they were moving across the subcontinent. The river Ravi, which flows very close to Lahore, provided them the calm they needed and the courtesans fulfilled their desires.

Baseer devoured the sights greedily. He hoped to see women

leaning against doorsills in anticipation, but to his dismay, the entire neighbourhood was as quiet as a graveyard. The 'businesswomen' had all relocated to posher parts of the city where the trade could be more profitable. Disappointed, he had moved on to see the other urban areas that were chock-a-block with buildings, lit-up restaurants and fragrant bakeries. He would not stop people on the roadside to show his merchandise; he just walked. In a place full of strangers, he trusted no one. So he decided to depend on the train that had carried him from the desert to this city. When he was done walking, he would go back to the station and sleep inside a deserted train bogey. He was mentally mapping the city. Every day, for a week, he went farther and farther within.

One of the most typical things of Lahore that Baseer got to witness was its social stratification—lowest, lower-middle, upper-middle and upper. On the seventh day, he had managed to wander into some of the most elitist areas of Lahore—Defence, Gulberg and Cantonment. The bungalows were breathtaking. White marble was used in abundance as if it cost peanuts and rocks and granite were polished and smoothened with such finesse that they made floors and walls shine like semi-precious stones that adorned the jewellery worn by the women back home.

Baseer had been eyeing the ladies in Lahore with interest, too. Their clothing changed just like the transformation of the buildings according to different localities. He had seen abayas and burkas with niqab, and shalwar qameez with dupatta or without. He had seen girls who wore a fiery shade of rouge

## Maria

on their cheeks and lips and dressed up like men, in pants and jackets. He saw women and men segregated by their sacred boundaries, in places like the waiting room of the station and vehicles of public use, but he also saw girls and boys sitting together on the pavements of Anarkali Bazaar or sipping coffee at the roadside cafes. He had not realized that some women had seen him ogling or leering and had turned up their noses in disgust. 'Jungli,' most had commented.

Ha, now that is funny! How wrong they were! He wasn't jungli—an ignorant wild animal—he was a caveman. Literally!

On the eighth day of his arrival, Baseer had seen most of the city of his dreams. But although he had walked through green gardens, he still had not found the tree of his imagination. There was a great poplar in Jinnah's Garden. Its trunk had the circumference of about five feet. He saw a young couple, both of them teenagers, walk up to it, and tie a colourful ribbon on one of its branches. Baseer didn't understand, as he didn't know that it was a tradition for lovers to go tie a ribbon on the poplar, as it was thought to bring good luck to their relationship. Or so the myth went. Despite its so-called magical powers for the love seekers, Baseer was not impressed.

A week had ended and Baseer had become aimless. He walked on the empty roads of Gulberg, a posh locality with its huge castle-like mansions, with people who had money drizzled down to them from their ancestral lands, businesses and scrupulous bank accounts. The money from such sources reflected well in the houses these people kept—large, spacious lawns in front, exotic flowers dotting the bright green ivy, or nasturtiums bordering one of the several walls of the 20,000 to 25,000-square-feet houses.

One such house with nasturtiums took Baseer's fancy and he squatted in front of it. The house towered like a fortress, high above the rest in the locality. The exterior had recently been painted a beige colour. Four sleek cars stood in the driveway, parked one behind the other, leaving just enough space for one person to walk.

Baseer didn't realize it, but he was standing there with his mouth hanging open at the grandeur of the beauty in front of his sight. That's when he was introduced to the lady of the house. She emerged like a vision from behind the tightly shut door, wearing a white dress with streaks of heather and lilac. Her shins were bare, and her steps were light in the flat silver pumps she had worn. The allure of the house was overshadowed by this exquisite creature that Baseer's eyes beheld. He was stupefied. Something glistened while he fed his eyes hungrily on her glowing legs; it was the mirrored sunglasses she wore. Without much ado, the gatekeeper who sat behind the iron gate, leapt up to clear the way for the car. A uniformed chauffeur offered his services but was turned down.

Baseer watched as the lady disappeared inside a white car and swooshed past him as if he were a mere pebble on the road. His heart missed a beat when the car took a turn on the dusty road and all he was left with was the cloud of dust he had, till then, taken so much pain to escape from.

That evening, Baseer did not bother to buy food. Any man who has been smitten, would know what Baseer was going through at that time. The glowing, white face of the woman he had seen from a distance—half of it covered with huge aviators—and her full form, had lit a fire inside of him. After getting sound sleep on the same berth of the hideous bogey for seven consecutive nights, he realized only that night, how uncomfortable the berth was. He heard sounds from the darkness that he hadn't been paying attention to all these days and blamed this and that for his lack of sleep. He wanted to go back to the desert and let his companions play the dutar for him for a while; he was agitated. He tossed and turned, until his sides were sore from all the movement.

As soon as the sun was out, Baseer gathered his carpets and throwing the rolls on his back, headed out for the same mansion. He sat in the same position as the day before and waited. Cars swooshed past, the sun broadened its grin and time passed. Baseer waited. His eyes yearned for a sight of the aphrodisiacal sight he had witnessed the previous day, but what he actually got to see was the old gatekeeper with a rifle hanging from his shoulder and a cheap mobile phone on which he listened to music with his earphones. It was sheer disappointment for him.

When the sun had set, he still wanted to wait. He spotted a yew tree at the end of the road and slumped against it. The lack of sleep had made him lethargic but he was determined to stay up in case the lady drove past. The darkness of the evening spread its wings farther and farther with every hour and during one such hour, his eyes closed and he fell asleep.

This pattern continued for a few days. He would stand, sit and walk around the block all day until one day, the gatekeeper asked him what his business was around the neighbourhood.

'Carpets,' he had replied.

The gatekeeper was confused by Baseer's terse response. Further interrogation revealed the 'business' of the loafer—he *sold* carpets.

'Can I see them?' the gatekeeper asked. He, too, was obviously bored.

Baseer had been frustrated since the past five days, looking only at the gatekeeper's face. But this was a good chance to go nearer to the threshold of the house. The patio was so inviting, with its cherry-blossom-coloured granite. The tall walls of the exterior were a perfect match for the floor, and the main door that led the visitor to the world inside, was made from walnut wood which was a shade darker than chocolate brown. He could only wonder what the beautiful woman must be doing behind that closed door.

'Oye!' The gatekeeper shook him out of his fanciful imagination.

Baseer, startled, went closer to the patio and started unrolling his carpets. One after the other, he spread them out like cloths from heaven, not allowing the guard to touch anything, but only to look. One had a vase, with gold threadwork upon a royal blue background, and a dozen roses which seemed to pour like a fountain. Another had a willow, with a flock of bluebirds, each sitting on a solitary branch. And the last one portrayed the shield of a warrior, which had patterns of black and red criss-crossed with silver threads, and two swords hanging on either side of it.

'How much for one?' the gatekeeper asked with interest,

*Maria*

although both of them knew he was not a potential customer.

'Seven thousand,' Baseer said in a very quiet voice.

'Seven? Are you out of your mind? This is not even a good size!' the gatekeeper exclaimed.

Baseer silently squatted and began to roll up his merchandise. He was done with two of them when he heard the knob on the walnut-wood door turning softly. Baseer's eyes shot up. The door opened and he saw her. Her movements weren't as quick as the first time; she took her time to pause and shut the door behind her. She wore a mauve sari and her shoes made a clicking sound as she walked. Her bare midriff and arms caught his attention and reignited the flame within him. She made eye contact with Baseer for a very brief moment and then looked at the uniformed chauffer who had come running to be of service to the lady. She seemed to be in her late thirties, though her slim, petite figure fiercely denied that age. Baseer saw her step down the patio, giving no regard to either him or his rugs as she slid into the gleaming car.

Baseer did not blink for even a single moment. He had gulped in the beauty of the woman in huge swigs. The trace of perfume she had left behind was manna to his desire. He was so overwhelmed by the moment that it was no more possible to keep squatting, and so he let himself sit on the cold floor. He found that his heart was racing and his lungs were devoid of air. The gatekeeper closed the gate as the car sped out. That was Baseer's cue to go back from where he had come and so he went and resumed his position at the yew, waiting for the car to come back.

If seeing the woman alone could suffice to keep him alive, Baseer could have done well. Unfortunately, the human body has needs. Now, the trees in the neighbourhood and the empty plot where the huge container of trash was kept by the municipality office allowed him to relieve himself, but he had to keep his stomach from merely grinding air. Once, every day, he had been living off the cob of corn a nearby vendor sold for a cheap price. The week-long loitering had not done the damage to his health that sitting under the tree of the dead had. His eyes had become sunken and his face seemed older. The stubble he had been proud of as a sign of manhood, had grown thicker and messier.

It was on the sixth day that Baseer reaped the fruit of his toil and misery. The lady of the house came to the gatekeeper, informing him of the arrival of some guests. She was in her night clothes—a t-shirt and shorts. Baseer, who had been slumping, had stood up hurriedly for a better view. He had never seen a woman half-dressed; this was scintillating for him. He saw her glance at him once, but her conversation continued with the gatekeeper.

A little while later, when she had floated back into the house with her light steps, the gatekeeper started walking towards Baseer.

'Madam wants to see you,' he said drily.

The thorns stuck in Baseer's throat suddenly came up to his tongue, and he felt he had no voice.

'She wants to see your rugs,' said the gatekeeper. He was not very happy about the proposal.

*Maria*

Baseer's eyes opened wide and he stared at the man, as if in a stupor.

'What? Are you deaf? Let's go inside! Pick up your crap,' shouted the gatekeeper, breaking his trance.

Baseer needed no second hollering. He went inside the house and climbed the step to the patio, when the gatekeeper hissed from behind, 'Shitface! Splash a little water on yourself. You look terrible!'

Baseer had bathed in a masjid's bathroom earlier that morning, so he ignored the gatekeeper, who knocked at the door and waited for a few seconds. Then he turned the knob and shoved the carpet seller inside.

Indoors, the place was a different world. The ground beneath his feet was covered with a plush cream carpet. His feet sank into it as he walked a few steps with trembling legs. In the middle of a huge expanse of a room were sets of sofas and couches, milky white with lilac cushions. In the middle of these, was a table composed of glass alone; the top, vertices and legs—pure, unbreakable glass. A chandelier hung from the ceiling. It was crystal clear the moment his eyes noticed it, but changed hues every moment—starting from blue, to cyan, pink, magenta, red, green, white and then back to blue.

Baseer was dumbfounded for multiple reasons. His feet were glued to the carpet as he looked around. From one of the rooms connected to this grandiose display of a sitting room, emerged the lady. Her hair fell loosely around her face. She had covered up in a saffron-coloured silk gown. The auburn hair around her cream-complexioned face was a vision to behold. Baseer looked at her like a small kid looks at fireworks for the first time.

She sailed through the room and settled on one of the settees, folded her legs one atop the other and signalled Baseer to come closer.

'Fyaz tells me you have Persian rugs to sell.'

Her voice was as smooth as the silk she wore. Baseer gathered that Fyaz must be the gatekeeper. He squatted on the floor beside her. Not blinking even once, he waited for further orders.

'Well? Let's see what you have.'

The salesman unrolled the carpets one after the other. He didn't know that the lady was noticing the flush on his face and the deepening colour of his ears and throat. As Baseer's carpets lay unwrapped on the spotless cream one of the house, she studied them all. She got up from her settee and ran her toes along the border of the vase and then the shield. She liked it a lot, she told him. He just stared back, petrified.

The woman was amused. She tried to hide a smile but the childlike awe of the young man in front of her made her pleasure irrepressible and she let out a small chuckle. Baseer was a little embarrassed. Did she know what thoughts ransacked his brain? Could she sense the turmoil in the pit of his stomach?

'What is your name, boy?' She wore a smile on her face.

'Baseer.' He spoke out the word in a choked voice.

'How old are you?' she asked.

'Twenty.' He had to think before replying.

'You are not from around, are you?' Her delicate hand caressed a loose strand of hair around her neck.

'No,' he managed to say. He would have gone further to tell her of the desert he came from, when a loud knock on the entrance door interrupted him. Both of them looked that way.

'What is it, Fyaz?' she called out.

Fyaz peeped in with half his head and one of his eyes visible. 'Asif Sahab is here,' he announced.

'So why are you making him wait? Send him in,' she said rather curtly.

'I am sorry Madam. I thought you were busy.' The man was really apologetic.

'With whom? Him?' She pointed at Baseer and let out an unkind laugh.

Baseer was still trying to analyse what had happened and what her words meant, when a tall man with dark hair walked in to the room. He looked like a foreigner of sorts. Well, at least to the simple Baseer, he looked like Indiana Jones, minus the hat. A buttoned-up, crisp white cotton shirt and wrinkled khakis on the tall man completed the Harrison Ford look on him.

Baseer noticed the lady smiling when he entered the room, and as she jumped off the couch to go embrace him, she let the loose knot of her silk gown untangle and reveal the fitted t-shirt she wore underneath and the moistened shins she had covered up earlier. Baseer was crushed when he saw them embrace in a way that her entire being had sunk into the lanky form of the stranger.

Baseer wanted to pull out the dagger that their hug had thrust inside his heart and stab the man with it instead.

'What are we doing, Maria?' the man asked, as both of them

snuggled together on the couch behind him.

'Why, Asif, do you like any of these carpets? They are Persian. And abrisham, this boy says so,' she purred.

That was a very trying moment for Baseer. While the woman's name sounded like honey to his ears, the pronunciation of the man's name from the lady burnt him up on the inside. While he was going through this emotional ride, Asif had already stood up and was looking at the three rugs with amused interest.

'How much for this one, boy?' He was squatting and running his fingers through the carpet with the pattern of the shield and swords.

Baseer had no intention of doing business with him. So he decided to up the ante.

'Twenty thousand.' He thought it was enough to put him off. 'Good riddance,' Baseer thought to himself.

'I will take it,' Asif announced, as he perched himself on the sofa, next to Maria. Baseer's jaw dropped. He had not expected this.

'Well, Baseer, that's a good deal.' Maria spoke to him as if she knew him well. Asif shifted a little in his seat.

'How long have you been selling carpets, boy?' Asif sat so close to Maria, that when he spread out one arm behind her across the sofa, she seemed to be enwrapped by him.

'Oh, he is new, I believe,' Maria answered for Baseer, still smiling at him.

Asif pulled out a cigarette case from his pocket and offered one fag to Maria. She accepted gladly.

'Here, boy.' Asif held out a wad of currency notes for

*Maria*

Baseer. It was an interesting scene to watch from a distance; a juxtaposition of cultures. It was the desert versus opulence.

'When you are done, leave the abrisham rug just there.' Asif's tone had suddenly become more authoritative.

Baseer kept his head down, accepted the money and started rolling the other two rugs.

Asif and Maria were conversing with each other as if they had already dismissed him. They spoke in a foreign language, kind of like the one in the *Indiana Jones* movies. All Baseer could gather was when Asif asked Maria, 'Where are the other girls?' and she stretched like a mountain cat before replying, 'Fia and Simi are in Dubai for the week and Lily is with a client.'

'The same guy?' Asif asked with interest.

'Yeah, I guess,' she said with indifference.

Baseer was all bundled up with his remaining two carpets and had no reason to stay. He stared at them both, smoking, talking. It was hurtful.

'Tell Fyaz to send the cook,' Asif told him. Baseer stood up and turned to go. His heartbreak was obvious from his face.

'Baseer?' he heard Maria purr from behind.

He turned to see her when she said, 'Come back tomorrow. I am short on cash today but I want to buy a carpet.'

This gave back his face some of its lost colour.

As he walked through the door, he heard Asif say, 'Since when have you been short of cash?' and Maria only giggled in response.

Time had become a bed of thorns for the carpet vendor. He couldn't stop himself from drifting to the thoughts of Maria with Asif. He waited all day for Asif's car to leave her house. Morning turned to noon and noon turned to afternoon. In the evening, just before sunset, when the love-bitten young man was forlorn with a broken heart, he finally heard a car rev up and speed down the curve of the road.

The next morning was still in its infancy when Baseer rang the bell. Fyaz came running.

'You? What do you want?' He wasn't pleased to see him.

'Maria asked me to come.' He tried to sound like Asif.

Fyaz stared back at him. He didn't quite understand. Since it was not his job to ask questions, he told him to wait and disappeared.

A few moments later, he opened the door and told him to go inside.

Maria was not in the magnificent sitting room. He looked around, waiting for her to appear.

'Baseer?' he heard her call out his name.

He froze.

'In here,' she called out again.

He followed her voice to one of the two rooms attached to the sitting room. The door of one was ajar and he peeped in it to see Maria, her hair tousled, still in bed.

'Come, come!' she urged, seeing that he was hesitant.

She was still under the bedcovers. He stared at her like a child stares at his favourite ice cream as it is being scooped out.

She laughed a gentle laugh, though he didn't know what amused her.

'So? Why are you here?' she asked in an all-knowing tone.

*Maria*

'I...I brought the carpets,' he stammered a little.

She laughed again. This time it was loud.

'Alright, let's have a look at them.' She sat up but was careful not to remove the covers from her body.

So Baseer did the job once again. He unloaded the bundles from his back and unrolled them. She looked at him with as much interest as she had looked at the carpets.

'I like the willow,' she said almost immediately. It was as if she had her mind made up already.

'You don't like the flowers?' Baseer pointed out the vase. If he could give a carpet as a present to her, it would be the one with the vase. It was symbolic of beauty, love and good luck.

The willow was a depiction of sorrow.

'You like flowers, eh?' she said.

He shrugged.

'I will take the willow. How much?' she reached out for a wallet at the nightstand.

Baseer was reluctant. He didn't want money. He had made enough from Asif.

'You can keep it,' he said.

Maria's face changed colours. Her hand dropped and she looked at him expressionlessly for quite a few moments. He was bewildered by her stare. But he chose to look back as if he deserved to lock eyes with her as much as Asif did.

When she blinked, she let out a small sigh.

'Come here, Baseer. Come sit next to me.'

He followed the orders.

'Tell me, do you have a woman?'

He looked puzzled.

'A girlfriend, a fiancée or a wife?' she explained.

He shook his head, not sure where this was leading.

She closed her eyes and sighed again.

When she opened them, she saw the innocence on Baseer's face. She wanted that innocence. She wanted that childish, awestruck gleam in his eyes. And since she was wanton, she pulled him close and taught him the art her profession had made her a master in.

෴

You know what happened, don't you? But you want it to be said out loud. What occurred between the two of them is what happens between lovers when their passions are flamed with solitude and temptation. What happened then, can be explained in many words of poetry. But this is not poetry. You will have to suffice by knowing they had crawled inside each other's spirit. He had gasped and ogled as she bared her soul to him. She laughed muffled laughs when his face darkened with embarrassment as he explored her nooks and crannies, her vales and mounts.

So were they lovers, one might ask.

To Baseer, it didn't matter what they were to each other. In those few moments, she had become the air in his lungs, the blood in his veins and the throb within his heart. Defining the relationship was no longer important.

Human connection doesn't go beyond that, does it?

As far as the lady, Maria, is concerned, well, to say the least, it didn't matter to her either, what they were to each other.

## Maria

She had shared the very sanctity of her bedroom with different men. They had all been diverse in form, name, social status and behaviour. The only thing that put them all in one category though, was they knew too much. They had women in their lives—girlfriends, lovers, wives. While with Baseer, such wasn't the case.

He had a starry-eyed look. All the while you have been seeing Maria as the temptress. But actually, it was she who was tempted. The flush in his ears, the blush on his cheeks, the gasps when he admired her beauty—it was all enticing to a woman who had grown used to biting the forbidden fruit.

After a while, with her appetite quenched, she sat on the edge of the bed. With her bare back towards Baseer, she picked her wallet, counted ten thousand rupees and threw them on the duvet. Baseer had been in a stupor—he thought he had finally reached the tree of his dreams and was lying under its towering presence, when realization dawned upon him. The tree was actually lying below his feet—the weeping willow on the rug that was spread under Maria's plush bed.

'You should go now,' she quietly said, lighting up a slim bar of rolled tobacco between her lips.

Baseer was dumbfounded. He immediately convinced himself that something must have gone wrong.

'Is he here?' he asked.

'Who?' she asked coldly.

'Your husband?'

'Who?' she turned around, her face twitching.

'Asif,' he paused. 'Your husband?'

She turned back and said softly, 'Well, he is someone's husband, of course,' and let out a puff of smoke.

Baseer's conscious mind brimmed with questions. He denied all the allegations his mind put up against Maria. He took quite a while, fighting a duel with the rising illusions, delusions, realities and revelations. He looked at the willow tree that seemed more tragic than before.

'Is this the only carpet you have to sell?' she stretched on the bed, staring at the ceiling.

Baseer did not understand why she suddenly wanted to talk about his carpets after all that had happened. He was too awed to even speak. Did it mean nothing to her?

'Well?' she prompted, sitting up again to dust off the ash from her cigarette. Baseer was trying to differentiate truth from hope. For a young man like that, you cannot expect him to be very calculative, can you?

'Can I see you again?' he asked her.

'For what?' she was still facing the wall, puffing away.

Baseer had a hundred replies to that question but he couldn't pick one out that sounded convincing enough to a woman who already had everything. How much weight could 'love' have for her?

'I want to see you again.' He pushed it one step further.

Silence. She stopped smoking. Baseer watched her hand as it drifted across the nightstand to crush the stub of the cigarette with full force.

Finally, she turned to face him. 'Why?' she asked.

'I would not be able to live without you,' he blurted out,

his eyes gaining a sheen.

Maria broke out in laughter.

'There is no such thing, Baseer,' she panted, when her guffaws had subsided. 'You will live when you will breathe and eat and drink. Oh, and sleep well. That, too,' she added hastily, like a physical trainer to his student. She turned to look at the mirror behind her. With the tips of her fingers, she smoothed out the frown lines above her brows. Baseer watched.

'Tell me, boy,' she still spoke without looking at him. 'Where are you from?'

'Kharan.' The heartbroken young fellow could hardly utter any words.

'Where's that?' She scrunched up her nose.

'Balochistan.' His voice was getting feebler.

'Oh, that's why you have carpets to sell. Well, you made good profit here, didn't you?' She winked at him. He was stabbed. The playful gesture would have taken him to newer heights if Maria hadn't been so ruthless in squeezing the life out of his heart.

'Listen to me, Baseer. Go back. There is nothing for a man like you here. You belong in the virginity of the maiden desert.'

'City life,' she sighed, 'it's just exhilarating in the beginning. You don't know the heartache it gives to you.' She reached out and touched his cheek with her hand.

'Too late,' he thought.

'I have to go in an hour, so you should leave now.' She stood up and signalled at the door.

He wanted to say farewell, but at the same time, he wanted to keep alive the hope of seeing her again.

He was ready to leave in a minute. He picked up the money, paused for a brief moment, put it back and exited the room.

'I want the carpet.' She rushed after him, seeing that he hadn't taken the currency notes.

'It's yours.' He pointed towards the spread-out willow tree under her bed.

'Then take your money.' She held the notes out to him.

He looked at her with soulful eyes, and turned back again.

She came running after him and screamed, 'What? You are going to judge me now? Judge yourself, boy! Take your shit with you!'

Baseer kept walking. He was too engaged keeping the million pieces of his broken heart together in his ribcage to pay attention to her tantrums.

On the way out, Fyaz looked at him with a sly smile on his face.

'She did it with you?' He was half impressed with the lad and half envious. Baseer chose to stay quiet. 'When did she tell you to come back, eh?'

Baseer thought for a while and told him he wasn't sure.

'Bloody slut,' Fyaz chuckled under his breath.

His words felt like a hammer strike somewhere inside his chest but he was too young to give up on the early notions of love.

He resumed his exercise to map the neighbourhood. Everywhere he went, he carried the lucky charm of the vase with him. He had lost interest in being a merchant for a while. He would stare at Maria's mansion many times in a day. Sometimes, he would see other girls coming in and out. Sometimes, he would see other men. Maria, too, would be seen. She would also look back but never sent a message through Fyaz again. His eyes never searched the length of her legs that were consciously left bare, or how much of her midriff was showing through the sari as she clung on to the shoulders of the men who took her away to be their arm candy.

Rather, he searched her face. Did she feel what he had felt after the fateful experience in her room? He was never fully able to read her expressions. She never gave away much. It wrenched his heart to know that she was oblivious to the idea of love or loyalty.

She never got him removed from her porch, either. It was as if she was trying him, to see how long her effect would take to wear off. She could not afford to have a persistent lover. But she was curious to see how potent her charm was.

Well, for a man who has been raised in the desert, persistence is second nature. He knew how to deal with annihilating sandstorms. Heartbreak was a new venture, but nonetheless, very close to a sandstorm. He sold off his third rug to someone in the same neighbourhood, without haggling for the price. His back was just sore with all the carrying-around.

~

The days grew colder in Lahore and Baseer was not prepared for that. He refused to stay away from Maria's house but the yew tree was not enough to shade him from the chilling blows of winter or the fog that encapsulated all of Lahore for the entire season, every year. Baseer needed clothes and shoes. He also needed a blanket. Most of all, he needed to eat and drink qehwa. He slept through the night in the masjid, but came out, as if on duty, as soon as he was up. One would think he was under a spell, but those who have been bitten by love, know that there is no enchantment stronger than it. Days turned into weeks, and before he knew it, he ran out of money. He went back to Kharan, penniless.

He brought shame to his family for not being able to return his uncles' money and his mother wouldn't talk to him for days.

'I trusted you,' she said when she finally forgave him and gave him her precious gold hoops to sell for another go at the carpet business.

'Don't tell your father,' she told him. 'Go quietly tonight.'

She sent him off to Sistan again. This time he afforded to buy two carpets and took his course to Lahore. He promised himself to not go to the neighbourhood where Maria could rip him of his sanity once more.

But promises are meant to be broken, aren't they?

Would you believe if you were told that it took him seven years to come out of the line of fire Maria had drawn around him? No? Ha!

He had slogged for seven years and his carpet business was no more dependent on his loitering, for he had set up shop in the marketplace.

Seven years is a long time, folks. He stopped standing in front of Maria's house, but she kept house in his heart. He quit longing for her, but she stayed in his subconscious mind when he made love to his wife who bore him four children. She will always

## *Maria*

have that influence on him...the kind of potent intoxication that wears off but can be stimulated with the slightest reintroduction.

Age had brought Baseer closer to the abrisham, the vase, the willow and the shield. This is what he had been eating, living and breathing every day, day in and day out, all these years. The rugs kept him connected to Sistan, Kharan and Maria. They kept him sharp and agile and the belly of his piggy bank, stuffed with currency notes. In all honesty, it is the rugs that kept him, and not the other way around.

# Summi
## *The soldier's wife*

The ravens were pecking on the ground, trying to split the partially cracked peanut shells. They had developed a taste for the salty, roasted nuts since they had been snacking on them at quite a regular schedule. The floor would have tiny prints of peanut shells, raven claws and beak-prints, once it dried. On the other hand, the ravens would have to whet their beaks and scrape the thin line of mud off their feet later on. This is because Summi, short for Summaiyya, had just finished covering the courtyard ground with a coat of golden-coloured, freshly dug-up soil mixed with a handful of hay. She had stepped into her bedroom—the singular room of her house—just to allow the courtyard to dry completely before lunchtime. The goo that coated her hands was wiped clean at the threshold of the bedroom. She ran her sight across the courtyard, and spotting the birds, shooed them away, renewing her vow to get a marble floor instead of new clothes that winter. She breathed out heavily—partially for her feeling of determination, and partially for being exhausted by an hour's labour. Summi went inside to check on her three-year-old toddler, Nadir.

The little boy was sleeping in his cane-woven basket. She smiled when she looked at his curled fingers and the curved thumb that was actively used as a pacifier. The tiny beep of the cell phone pulled away her motherly gaze from Nadir. It was Murad. The smile changed and turned into a lover's shy beam. Murad was more of a long-distance lover than a husband. He was a soldier in the cantonment near Waziristan. It had been four years since the war on terror had begun in Pakistan and during this time, Murad's family had managed to get him married to a girl from the clan. What they couldn't do, was to make him stay. His visits were frantic, short and much coveted by his wife.

'You will call, won't you?' the new bride had wistfully asked her husband as she saw him packing just the day after their wedding. Murad, sitting on the edge of the charpoy they had just shared and woken up from, was tying up his military boots. He looked up only to meet a pair of shy eyes that glanced down. Colour rose to her cheeks as he whispered a promise in her ear to stay in touch.

And so he did. The beep that day had revealed the romantic facet of the tough-hearted soldier—a verse from Rumi, a line from Attar—anything that could keep the flame burning between the long-distance lovers. The colour of Summi's cherry-red cheeks deepened as she read the text message:

*I choose the path of love, so I choose you.*

Her romantic moment was interrupted by a sound of wings flapping impatiently and the caw-cawing alarm of the frustrated birds who would not give up on the red-skinned nuts that refused to budge from their shells.

'Haaiee!' she said, trying to shoo them away from the slits of the window.

The ravens cawed back. She threw a slipper at them, which made them fly away and perch themselves upon the courtyard walls. They were looking for a last chance to have a go at the incomplete meal, but finally flew away, spitting curses in the form of their hoarse shrieks. The commotion had woken the baby. Nadir, meaning brave in the local Pushto language, was half her world. The other half was, of course, away on duty. She brought him near to her bosom. Comforted, the wails subdued and the tiny mouth went back to suckling on the thumb.

Summi sang a soft lullaby and gently cradling him, put him back into the crib. The room was miniscule and its furnishings, minimalistic—a bed whose mattress was a duvet-like structure filled with cotton wool, a white bedcover that was lined along the edges with tiny, embroidered magenta flowers (with a bigger print of the same pattern on the pillows), matching curtains and a dresser. The mirror was smallish but the dresser served Summi well, for it was used to stack her trousseau, Nadir's baby stuff and her limited collection of cosmetics. There was a kohl liner that her maternal uncle had brought from the border between Lahore and India. She had particularly asked for the one that she watched in TV commercials. Another was the floral perfume that Murad had gifted her the last time he was here. He had boasted of it being of a higher value than other ittars and oudhs, for it was bought off an Afghan Hazara trying to illegally cross the porous border shared with Afghanistan.

'Did you let him through?' Her eyes were wide with amazement when Murad told her the anecdote.

'Of course. Why not? He is just a Hazara like us. He had no weapons. Just two little daughters with him. I felt sorry,' Murad went on with the tale. He was justifying to his wife why he had been lax in the line of duty. It was a win-win situation since he was aware his wife would place him on a higher pedestal for not just being kind, but also having a heart of solid steel for defying the orders from his battalion commander. And while he did that to gain a more heroic stature in her eyes, he was trying to convince himself of his chivalry, too. Lying on the charpoy in the courtyard, he was tossing peanuts to the neighbour's geese, and chewing on some hay. While he basked in the sunny admiration of his wife, who thought of him as the bravest soldier in the land, he couldn't help but shy away from her gaze, for he knew he had done little to earn that hero-worship from Summi.

He couldn't wipe the image of the old Hazara man with two teenage daughters on each side, both of them having pulled an edge of their cloaks over their faces. The old man's back arched with the load of the camp beds that he carried; greying hair and an even more grey beard, shaggy blue khet partug, or the afghan robe, on his body, and his glassy, grey eyes dimmed with a broken pride—the frailty in his composition was enough to thaw the frozen ground beneath his feet, but certainly not enough to mellow the border patrol regulations.

'Think of your father,' he pleaded. Murad had looked away. Both daughters tugged at his arms when they saw that the soldier won't budge.

'Come, father…' They had gently encouraged him to turn back. Murad had shamefully looked at them. Although both girls had only made their eyes visible through the cloaks, Murad didn't miss the hurt and hate written in big, bold letters in them. He had fabled about his opulent gift to Summi. The old man could not have offered Murad the riches of the world to let him pass. He shared so much with the refugee—culture, heritage, history, origins, language and demographics. Yet, he couldn't help him. There was a lot more than a twisted, barbed wire that lined the border. There was a firewall of governmental orders, geostrategic policies and cantonment discipline to be followed.

Murad had turned his face away, not because he was indifferent; he was far from it—he was ashamed. But Summi didn't have to know that. She should keep alive her dream of being married to the boldest soldier. The truth was, her precious bottle of perfume was obtained from an Afghan border policeman, in exchange for a packet of cigarettes.

'It's a fine scent,' Murad had told Abbas, the Afghan soldier. It confused him as to how anyone could part with such a keepsake.

'Of course, it is fine,' he had retorted. 'What, you don't want it?'

'No, no, I do.' Murad was quick to pocket the bottle since his 'business partner' had already put a lit cigarette in his mouth. There was no point in giving up the exchange now.

'My girlfriend gave it to me,' Abbas explained a few minutes

*Summi*

later, having smoked a couple of fags.

'Why are you selling it like this?' Murad felt guilty. It was a lover's memento.

'Would you rather not smell nice on this desert patch in the middle of nowhere and share a cigarette with a brother?'

Murad smiled. He knew the answer to that one and the barter seemed fair. They both grinned and clasped each other's hand from between the barbed wires that separated Afghanistan from Pakistan.

'What makes you smile?' Summi ran a finger across his lips. She had been sitting on the edge of the wooden frame of his bed. While Murad had been lost in his soul-searching memoirs, she had unscrewed the bottle of ittar and had generously sketched crooked lines of the saffron-coloured liquid on her bare wrists and arched neck.

'You do.' He turned to her.

To Summi, Murad was no less than a superhero—the uniform, the weapons, the artillery, the stories—it was all fascinating.

It is a tradition to marry young boys with their female cousins in the tribal areas of Pakistan. Murad and Summi, too, were cousins. However, the time-worn tradition hadn't allowed them to see each other for more than a decade. When Murad's ageing grandmother had told him that Summi would be his bride, he had delved into the deeper recesses of his memory to bring to the top of his cognition, a girl of nine or ten, broken front teeth and oiled hair twisted into two long braids on either side of her small head. Her most attractive feature was a pair of leaf-green eyes, with specks of bottle-green on the iris. (Murad had recited poetry about her eyes on the wedding night.) She had a buttony nose and a thin strip of a mouth, which parted to reveal what was considered a sign of adulthood in girls—darkening gums. That's when the girl would be ready to hit puberty; thus, a marriageable age. The cap on her head sat like an overturned nest. It was rather opulent—rows of one-inch mirrors sewed with multicoloured thread, shells and beads to make patterns of flowers, peacock feathers and paisleys. Her long black robe wasn't any less rich in detailing. Bigger motifs with beads, shells, mirrors and dyed feathers adorned her robe, adding colour and glamour.

'Aren't you pleased?' His grandmother had tugged on the corner of his shirt when she saw him lost in thought. The young man of twenty-one hung his chin over his breast and smiled shyly. That was considered approval from the groom. He had informed all his friends in the cantonment through his social media handle, about getting engaged, and had grinningly accepted the congratulatory messages from the entire battalion. The Frontier Corps, a paramilitary force that Murad worked for, was assigned the duty of border patrol on the western precincts of Pakistan, adjoining Afghanistan. With the war on terror going on in the latter, refugees had an unquenchable desire to enter Pakistan. The Hazaras who were trying to cross the border that day, were from western Asia and had Mongolian ancestry. Their faces were reflective of their ancient heritage. Murad, a Hazara, too, had Mongoloid features along with a thin line of moustache above his upper lip.

## Summi

Even after the wedding ceremony had been held, Murad had yet to see his bride's face. A basin of copper was produced from an old lady's collection, was filled with clear water and rose petals were floated on it before stashing the basin between the newly married couple so they could see each other's reflection. Murad had winked and Summi had reddened within the huge ghoonghat, or veil, that was covering her head and forehead.

⁓

She had blushed when Murad bore his eyes into her face as they sat on the charpoy and would have made more of the moment had a frail wail from the baby waking out of slumber not cracked up the intensity of the moment. As Summi went inside to pick her baby from the cot, Murad stretched, waiting for his wife to bring the child to him whom he fondled for a few minutes and then announced that he was going to meet some friends.

Summaiyya smiled when she saw him off but was a little disappointed for she had expected him to be more generous with his time and attention when he came to visit her.

He is with friends at the border, she thought sadly. But love overcame the gloom almost immediately. It had suddenly occurred to her that Murad had no friends left in the vicinity. Some had abandoned the valley to go elsewhere with their families, and those who had chosen to stay behind...well... were few and far between. She knew exactly where he had gone. The understanding of her husband's mission made her gently nod her head. His excursion was necessary.

Murad had stepped out of the house and into the street. He

inhaled deeply. Not much had changed in the environs since his last visit. Well, not too much except the new, polished green door that his immediate neighbour had set up in place of the old, weather-beaten one. He had replaced wood with iron, giving his house the look of a dungeon. Murad shook his head. The street presented the same scene since the time he himself was a boy—a group of children from the neighbourhood playing cricket in uneven teams. They took turns to field, bowl and bat. Everything was pretty much the same.

The fourth house down the lane certainly had put up new curtains on the windows facing the road. He kept walking on the soft, soiled lane until he reached the last house and then took a turn to the left to reach the main road. His final observation made him sigh a little. This particular house was exactly the same. As always, the entrance door was collecting cobwebs and dust and there were muddy streaks made by raindrops. He noticed a trail of termites making little, strangely shaped hillocks on the surface of the door, which was, by now, probably hollow from within, for the protruding termite mounds seemed sturdier than the wooden planks themselves. Murad had known the inside of this house like his own, all through his childhood, adolescence and adulthood. It was his best friend Nadir's residence. He knew Nadir wasn't indoors. But he knew who was. Although he tried very hard to convince his feet to keep moving, his heart rebelled. He knew his short visit home would be burdened with guilt if he didn't go inside. His cognition also argued with his emotional urge, that the lingering sadness that would be the result of going down the path of hurt, would overshadow his days with Summi.

## Summi

But what had to be done, had to be done. So he pushed the door with the tip of his index finger. It wasn't locked, and that was no surprise. It opened wide, creaking like the joints of an old man waking up from slumber. The courtyard was messy— there were dry leaves from earlier windstorms and dust had gathered all over. The only room had its door ajar but no one was in sight.

'Amma!' Murad called out. He waited for a response. An old woman, around seventy, bent back, dry white hair framing her face like strands of wire, wrinkled skin hanging loose from her chin, cheeks and neck, and sunken eyes that gaped wide, peered out of the room.

'Nadir?' she croaked in a voice hoarsened by age, but crisp with hope.

'Yes, Amma.' Murad was ashamed to nod in the affirmative. He could never be Nadir. He could never deserve to be called by that name.

'Why so late, my son? I have been waiting and waiting,' her motherly complaint was filled with love, exasperation and relief.

'I... I had work to do,' Murad stuttered a little. He wasn't sure whether pretending to be Nadir was more cruel to the neurotic little lady, or telling her off.

'Okay wait, I will heat up the food for you.' She started taking quick steps towards the mound of plastered sand with the clay oven used for making bread and the hand-built stove with firewood, for cooking.

'I just ate...' Murad wondered if she even had anything to cook with.

'Stay quiet!' Her chide was motherly, with an air of

what-do-you-know-about-eating-well-unless-I-have-fed-you.

She stepped up on the mound with a difficult, forward lunge, and sat down near the clay oven to prepare fresh flatbread for her 'son'. She suddenly looked around, as if confused. Her psyche had taken her back to a time when Nadir's tapping footsteps at the door meant that she had to roll out a rounded flatbread that would be stuck to the walls of the oven to bubble up and get brown mounds—a sign of it being ready to be devoured.

She looked around to find no dough which had risen, no firewood, no heat from the hearth and no pot bubbling away on the stove.

'These kids from the neighbourhood...' she grumbled. 'I am telling you Nadir, this is their doing. They tease me all day with their silly games. Sometimes, they pour water in the oven, sometimes they try to hit me with a ball—and so fast is that ball, I tell you—if it touches my skull, my brain will come trickling out...'

'Amma, it's alright...' Murad tried to calm her down.

'No, sonny, you have to take me from here! Take me to where you work. I am very terrified here.'

'No one's going to hurt you, mother.' Nadir had taken a seat beside her. Cross-legged, he was trying to assure the forlorn woman that she was being unnecessarily paranoid.

'Why do you care? You don't write to me! You don't visit me! I am going to die someday but think of your fiancée. That poor girl! Why don't you come home for good? Get married! I want my own grandchildren playing with a wooden ball...' She was rambling on and on about all her fears, desires and complaints. She wanted to be heard after years and years of solitude, of yearning and desolation.

'As you say, Amma.' It was one of the most uncomfortable moments for Murad.

'You stay here. I will go fetch some firewood. I don't know where all of it went. Thieves are all around me. I don't trust anyone,' she grumbled, trying to stand on her feet.

'No, Amma, don't go! I am not hungry,' said Murad, trying to stop her from going through the tedious exercise of walking down the mound again. She needed to get her breath back before engaging in further physical activities. In his quest to make her settle down, he held her wrist. The old lady sat down with a huff. Her small, beady eyes, with discoloured pupils and bags of purplish skin hanging beneath, bore into his face.

Murad knew what was coming.

'You scoundrel!' The white-haired woman gasped in bitter spite. 'You are not Nadir!'

She looked around to pick up whatever she could to defend herself; anything—a gadget, a tool, a plate, a piece of coal.

'Where is my son? Where is he?' Reality had bared itself in front of her in its most malicious form. Mentally, she was back at the bus stop, looking for her son amidst the blood-splattered corpses and the gore-coloured faces that all seemed the same. The Mongoloid flat nose, the small eyes, the short eyelashes, the thin lines of moustache…they all looked similar when lined up for identification on the ground, and the wailing mothers, wives, brothers and fathers clutched at the lifeless bodies, staring at them with bewildered eyes.

'WHERE IS HE?' She was screaming now, and turning things over, throwing the utensils in different directions as if her son lay buried under the debris of her messy kitchenette.

Murad closed his eyes and stood near the door. The ruckus the lady was creating had attracted the neighbours' attention and he could see a couple of eerie-looking faces ogling through the slit of the entrance door. The kids who were playing cricket outside, had gathered to see the lunacy on display.

'GO!'

She screamed so hard that it took her breath away and she had to hold on to the wall to keep standing. Murad stepped out, but not without colliding with the kids outside. This wasn't the plan.

Murad had wanted to pretend being Nadir for a while and check on her. He then intended to leave after making an excuse, still pretending to be Nadir. But his touch, unfamiliar and strange to the mother, had triggered off a memory in her head. The fateful recollection of Nadir and twenty other Hazaras being shot in a bus, had come alive. The killers had asked everyone's names before shooting them for being Hazaras. Nadir and Murad were going off to the city to watch the Hollywood blockbuster, *Mission: Impossible—Rogue Nation*. Nadir had gotten on the bus five minutes earlier, and Murad, as usual, was running late. It had been Nadir's job since their childhood to put the bus conductor on hold for a few more minutes, to request the teacher to not mark Murad absent for he would reach the school 'in just a minute', and to plead to the boys on the street to wait a little while longer before beginning the match so that Murad could

## Summi

have his turn, too. So that day as well, Nadir was saving a seat for his soldier friend. His holidays were so sparse, and they both had been fans of the movie franchise.

However, that day, Murad's unpunctuality saved him the pain of having bullets pierce his face and chest. And Nadir's loyalty cost him his life.

This is how Murad saw it. He yanked back his head to see Nadir's mother in a frenzy, throwing things around and yelling. She was still calling out to Nadir, but the shrieks would subside after sometime when she would realize that he wasn't there. Grief would turn into passivity and through that, delusion would be born. She would wait for Nadir and that hope kept her going. While ducking his head to avoid the glares and stares of the onlookers, Murad took hurried steps towards his house and carried in his heart a lump of guilt and sorrow. He needed Summi to tell him what a hero he was. That was his psychological lifeline.

Summi's heart leapt as she heard a slight tap on the door—Murad's signature knock. She was squatting in front of the municipality tap, washing Nadir's soiled clothes. She jumped up, wiped her hands with the edge of her scarf and ran towards the door. The courtyard had been polished the day before and she had swept it with a broom in the morning. The smoothness of the floor was such that, from a distance, it might have looked like a fawn-coloured carpet had been spread along the length of the courtyard. Summi left wet footprints on the floor, as she opened the door to see a pale faced Murad, who hurriedly entered the house and shut the door behind him. It was as if he was running from assassins.

Summi was perplexed.

'What's wrong?' she asked, cupping her beloved's face in both her hands.

He looked at her face and saw the love. He couldn't say a word but his eyes welled up. He couldn't cry in front of the woman who called him brave. He turned away, walked into the room and shut it from inside.

Summi clamped her hanging jaw shut. She closed her eyes and sighed a little. 'Alas,' was the only word she could say.

Murad didn't come out until after sunset.

In the evening, Summi asked him if he would like to take the dinner tray for Amma, and he declined quietly. So she did the ritual herself. Summi wore a veil over her precious frock and held a tray in her hands—soft porridge cooked with lentils, onions and tomatoes, with a kettle of mint tea. Across the street, the door was ajar and the old, witchy lady was nowhere to be seen.

'Amma?' Summi called out.

'Nadir?' someone asked from inside the only room.

'No, Amma. It's me, Summi. I have brought dinner.'

Silence.

She carried the tray inside, where the old woman was sitting up, beaming for once.

'Summi, do you know? Nadir came to see me today.'

'Really? That's great!' Summi feigned surprise. She knew what had happened. Without any further comments, she scooped a spoonful of the mushy cereal and fed the lady. She didn't stop to chew and swallow, and kept talking between the

## Summi

bites. Summi kept listening like she always did, twice a day, every day.

'He brought me firewood. And we had lunch together. He was looking so handsome, my son. Have you seen him in those grey clothes of his? He looks like a prince. He has gone to the city with Murad. To the cinema. He asked me to go, too. Naughty kid, that one. I asked him, "What do I have to do with these frivolities?" He will be back. Is Murad back yet? No, of course not. They left together. They will come together. Summi, get me some firewood. I have to get dinner ready for him...'

Summi listened to the rattle with a smile plastered on her face. Murad hadn't told her anything, but the old woman's narration had given her enough insight into the day's event. Once her job was done, she tucked the old woman in bed and recited some holy words before ritualistically blowing atop her forehead.

Every morning she came to fill the water pots for Amma. As the clean spring water gushed from the hand pumps installed in every house, she dreaded seeing the old woman dead.

'It has to come, that day...' She tried to console herself daily, when the fears arose. Words happen to be the strongest suit of mankind, so words managed to calm her down as she pushed open the termite-ridden door each day. At times, the lady would be sitting at the threshold of the house, waiting for Nadir. At other times, she would be too weak to even climb out of the jute bed. Either way, she expected Summi both in the morning and at night, to feed her and pull the sheet over her legs as she lay down to sleep.

Having performed the ritual that evening, Summi collected her utensils and left the old woman to her nostalgic repression. She had a baby to tend to. If he had woken up, she was sure Murad must have been doing a good job. And she was quite right, for when she reached the entrance of her house, the door opened with a slight nudge of her elbow. The two most important beings of her life, Murad and Nadir, were in front of her eyes; her husband cradling her baby, smiling both at him and her, as he gently rocked the little being. She stopped in her tracks because the warmth of the scene in front of her eyes had entered her like a ray of sunshine, and the heat from her emotions oozed out of her through the radiance in her eyes, the flush on her cheeks, the glow on her face and the giddiness in the pit of her stomach.

'I shall leave in the morning,' he whispered gently to her when she came closer.

Summi did not say anything but her heart broke a little, just like it always did. She looked up at him and saw that he wore a strange expression; his eyes boring into her face. He saw that she was puzzled and tucked a loose strand of her hair behind her ear.

'You are amazing, you know that?' he told her in a whisper. She only smiled in return, thinking he was again flirting with her, admiring her beauty, when in actual, he was in awe of her bravery and courage. He could not believe how tactfully and lovingly she dealt with the mad old woman.

The experience he had had earlier in the afternoon would stay with him for a longer time than he would have wanted it to. But in Summi's case, she saw the old woman every day. She clothed her, fed her and put her to bed. She dealt with her lunacy on a regular basis. One day if she was easy to handle, the next day her hysterics would be uncontrollable. Yet, he never heard Summi complain. His wife was bearing the burden of his guilt. While she sang songs for him for being the bravest soldier in the land, she outsized him in valour, spirit and selflessness. The realization made him feel smaller than he had felt while turning away the old Afghan.

In the wee hours of the next morning, Summi had fed him, packed his bag and had sent him off after reciting Koranic verses and directing them towards his head and chest with a wave of her hand. The bus could pass through his hometown, anytime between daybreak to an hour after that. He had to wait in the makeshift shed-like structure the locals used as a bus stop. It was the same place where Nadir must have waited for him, all this time ago when he was brutally massacred. He was lost in the memories of his best friend, imagining how he must have endured the pain of being shot in the face and neck. Just then, the ravens, being early risers, flew past him. Their cawing sounded familiar. They were looking for some crumbs of food that the human in the shed may have dropped while he stood there. He watched the ravens sit on the ground, engaged in a meeting. Not having found anything to feed on, they cawed away, spitting abuse just like Amma had done the previous day.

# Habiba
### *The girl with topaz eyes*

*H*abiba hardly felt her frail hand burning against the scorching rock, as all her senses were mesmerized by the scene in front of her eyes. The prisoner had just been brought in, his body covered in a teal green burka and his feet tied together. Her brother and father—well-built, tall Pukhtoon men, who themselves had donned their rustic robes, with matching turbans on their heads—had dragged him out of the 4x4 jeep and hauled him inside a camel-leather tent.

Habiba had been watching the scene from behind the rocky mountain that separated her home from the place where his father kept his captives. There had been fewer hostages lately, but each time, Habiba made sure she witnessed their arrival. She had been lurking behind the rocks ever since she had heard the hum of her father's vehicle as it jumped over dunes and the rocky Jamaldini road that led to the dusty plain in the suburbs of the district of Nushki, where they had set up an abode for themselves—a couple of tents lined with all sorts of leather and linen to keep out the sun. One was sanctioned to herself and her elder sister, Ayesha. The other was used by her father and brother to sleep on alternate nights. This is because if one would sleep, the other would keep watch on the tents of the captives and the girls.

The expanse of the land inhabited by the family was separated from the closest village by at least twelve miles. The plain was hedged between a cliff and the rickety road that led to the outskirts of Nushki, and eventually, to the Durand Line, the porous border between Balochistan and Afghanistan. Their tents had been perched on one side of the plain, backed by the cliff. The captives' tents had been set up on the other side with another cliff at the back. But Sikander, Habiba's brother had taken the pains to erect a makeshift wall of rocks between the two portions of the land. It was to keep purdah, so that while the captives were out strolling for exercise or eating their once-a-day meal, they shouldn't be able to cast a glance on his sisters.

A man from any other culture would not have worried since his teenaged sisters were covered from head to toe in their traditional firaq partug—a long robe made with linen and embellished with kandahari doozi, an Afghan embroidery done with satin and silk threads and mirrors or sequins. Black trousers covered their legs down to their ankles, and the chador they wrapped around their head and bosom was sometimes also wrapped around half their face. If it were not for the markings of the delicately-patterned henna on their dainty feet, one would have trouble deciphering whether the person under the veil was a man or a woman. Due to the heat and sunshine, sometimes men, too, had to pull a corner of their turbans across their faces, just like her father had while he pulled at the captive like a sack of coals and thrust him inside the tent.

Habiba had been committing a forbidden act—going too close to the wall of purdah to watch the arrival of the new captive. She could not see his face, but like most of them, he, too, had stayed silent, sans any protest. What Habiba did not understand at the age of fifteen, was that they knew it would be of no use to scream or call for help in the midst of this barren land, among towering cliffs, in a realm where human population was as scarce as an oasis in a desert. Without any careful brainwashing or coercing, the spirits of the captives were broken as soon as they realized that even if someone slaughtered them in broad daylight, the desolate, cracked-up soil would soak up their blood even before the vultures got to smell the reek of the gore.

There had been instances when a troublemaker had to be put to his final rest in order to bring the others under discipline. Habiba remembered the white man. He was around sixty and her father had gotten the contract to take him from his residence in Lahore. She remembered the day he was brought in the same manner as the new captive—all bundled up in a burka, masking tape on his mouth. He had angrily shouted at them for hours when they had removed the tape. Habiba's father, Rustom, had given him ample time to cool down and let off steam. Sikander had motioned towards the Kalashnikov several times when his father glanced at him, but each time Rustom shook his head.

## Habiba

'Guest,' Rustom said, trying to pacify his hot-headed son. To them, as per strong Pukhtoon tradition, the captives were their guests. The father-son duo and Rustom's nephew, Bashir, also his aide, sat down on the ground at midday, right after they had brought the new 'assignment' and had washed their hands and faces in the small tub of well-water Habiba had brought for them.

Rustom had brought seekh kebab for his children. He had grown particularly hungry as he crossed Punjab and entered Quetta. When the tide seemed safe, he had stopped at the first kebab shop and ordered challo kebab and lamb seekh. Having eaten his share, he wrapped the rest in a bit of old newspaper and stuffed the package in the pocket of his khet partug.

He had offered a naan stuffed with minced lamb to the abductee with him, who was covered under layers of burka. The old man's hands were taped together and folded under the clothes, his feet were tied, his mouth was taped, too, and Rustom's accomplice, his nephew, had positioned a pistol at his ribs. Bashir and the prisoner sat in the back seat of the jeep and they had crossed thirty-five check posts between Lahore and Nushki, all of which they had passed easily due the cultural stronghold of the burka. For the mightiest of the military would dare not ask a Muslim woman to lift her veil — a demand which would be sinful at too many levels.

After eating, Rustom had resumed his task of driving them all safely to the plain on the mountain top. After securing the automated locks of all the doors of the jeep, he had instructed his nephew to lift the burka of the old man and give him some of the naan to eat. Once the tape from his mouth was removed, the old man spurted a stream of abuse at Rustom and his nephew. Although the language he spoke was beyond them, they understood he was insulting them filthy. He had to go hungry as a fresh band of tape was wound around his mouth so that the two kidnappers did not have to listen to foreign abuses the rest of the way.

The tiring journey was almost six hundred kilometres from where he had picked up the captive. He was American; maybe that is why he was of interest to his kidnappers. Whatever the reason, Rustom had learnt from his father, and had taught the same to his son, Sikander, that in their line of work, they need not ask unnecessary questions. They got paid for whatever risks they had to take and that kept the gunny sack in Ayesha's tent filled with flour to make bread. That is enough for a wild man of the desert. As basic as it may sound to the rest of the world so drenched in opulent desires, to keep the fire in the belly sprinkled with dough was literally enough for some in the world. Maybe a linear philosophy of life is what made them fearless, stoic and merciless. They wouldn't think twice before removing a defector from another clan or even their own.

The old American knew a lot of things about the tribal men who kidnapped people like him for ransom. What he didn't know, however, was that these tribals hated being rude.

Even after the American had been slipped into a regular khet partug and enchained to the rock like other abductees, he had kept yelling at Rustom. The reason why Rustom was quiet to the tantrums of the old man was that he did not, in reality, have any answers to his questions: Why was he kidnapped?

## Habiba

Who wanted him kidnapped? What is the ransom?

Rustom let the old man rant for hours. In the evening, the other seven captives in adjoining tents had started to speak up, too. They had been calling Rustom and his son, names. They had been jingling the chains on their feet as if they were trying to break them off. Sikander had twice gone to fire aerial shots to scare them but the old man had given the kind of courage to the inmates that only a leader can. They had convinced themselves that they could not be silenced by a gun since their lives ensured ransom for Rustom.

How wrong they were.

In the evening, when Ayesha had served her father and brother with their daily nightcap—a steaming cup of qehwa—Rustom signalled Sikander to go inside the tent. He put the cup full with qehwa on the ground and lifted his precious Kalashnikov when Rustom forbade him from picking up the weapon. Sikander obeyed and went inside his tent, although it was not his turn to sleep. Rustom took his cup for the old man who was sitting on a rocky surface, hitting the chains on his feet with a brick-sized rock to break them.

Rustom offered him the beverage, for the old man had refused to eat lunch and Rustom knew that he must be unwell from all the hectic trevelling, hunger, shock of being kidnapped and his constant hammering on the chain. The old man accepted the warm cup from his abductor and as Rustom was about to sigh with relief, a hot liquid was splashed on his face. It startled him for an instance, but it enraged him no end. Before either of them could think much, Rustom had angled the Kalashnikov on his shoulder and shot the abductee's brains out.

Sikander, Ayesha and Habiba had come running to the sound of the weapon as Rustom fired very seldom. That was one instance when Habiba and Ayesha had gone beyond the wall of purdah to witness the first dead man in their surroundings. They had both gaped, open-mouthed and wide-eyed, at the lifeless body of the old man who had been creating a ruckus all day and all evening. It was shocking to see him go quiet all of a sudden. The girls were both sent off, while Sikander helped his father to bury the sacrificial lamb. The other seven detainees caused no problem after that.

Now, Rustom had learnt his lesson. He had made a note to not treat the abductees too nicely. They had to be put in place immediately so that they didn't get ideas about taking up the role of a freedom fighter against him. It was this 'policy' that had made him throw the new captive into solitary confinement, his feet enchained to a metal hook dug deep into the rocky wall. The burka was then taken off, the tape removed from his mouth and he was given a bowl of water to drink.

✺

Habiba had burnt the palm of her hand against the oven-hot rocks as she craned her neck to get a concise look of the new man. He was terrified of her father, she could see that. Sikander, too, was trying to prove his manliness by slapping the abductee on the back of his head for no reason. Squatting on the rocky ground, his face wore mixed expressions of confusion, bewilderment and fear. He was nothing like a Pukhtoon—his

## Habiba

complexion was brown and his hair was dark. Pukhtoons were usually very fair-skinned with light eyes and hair. There was a mystery in his face, and his present, pathetic demeanour made him seem pitiable to Habiba.

She saw that her father and brother's job in terrifying the new captive was done, and they were walking towards the 'residential' portion of the area. She paced back to her tent, where Ayesha was sleeping.

'Ayesha, wake up!' Habiba tugged at her sister's sleeve. 'Baba is here,' she hissed in such urgency as if she had seen a ghost.

Ayesha, too, sat up and straightened her clothes—a long black frock whose hem reached her toes, adorned with mismatched embellishments and embroidery. The girls had to make do with anything that was available. They were simple desert girls but still had their sense of panache. Habiba fixed her shawl properly on her head and pulled at one end of the scarf to wrap it around her face in a manner that only her eyes were left bare.

At fifteen years of age, Habiba's beauty had not yet been admired by a man's eyes. She always had every bit of her skin covered; except her eyes—they were like a poetic mix of blue and green, with specks of gold and black in them. The tiny flecks made her eyes glitter. When she blinked them, they seemed to sparkle. The colourful eyeballs shone like topaz, and as she wore a veil on her face, the beauty of her eyes came out stark naked.

With her jewel-like eyes, she walked out of her tent, followed by her elder sister Ayesha, and greeted her father who patted her head in response. Her cousin and Rustom's accomplice, Bashir, had driven off with the jeep. Sikander had followed his father into the compound, his precious Kalashnikov on his shoulders, but almost immediately, dutifully turned back to go and see what activity was going on in the detainees' compound. Habiba grimaced at him for she knew he was trying to act all bossy in front of their father. She was quite fed up with her brother's domineering conduct, especially in Rustom's absence.

Sikander was going through a phase. He was fourteen, had entered puberty and his raging testosterone was irritating him a lot. He was particularly upset about why his father wouldn't allow him to go on kidnapping expeditions. He was furious at Bashir for being his father's wingman, when that place actually belonged to him. He should be the one getting trained for being the future master-kidnapper and not his paternal cousin. He was done with playing bodyguard for his two silly sisters who didn't need any guarding anyway. They were lazy lasses who spent most of their time in the tent sewing or making henna patterns on each other's hands and feet.

Sikander had been asking his father to wed the girls off so they could be free to do whatever they wanted. The prospect of sleeping every night seemed like a dream to him, which was quite achievable once his sisters would be burdens of their husbands, and not his.

Sikander was younger than his sisters but his gender, as per tradition, gave him an upper hand over them; hence, the bossiness. While Habiba's interest in the new captive was formed out of curiosity, Sikander had made a silent vow to himself to manage the new captive himself, to prove to his father that he had grown into a fine and strong young man and was well-equipped to take the place of Bashir.

Rustom was not yet ready to take his son as his aide. He was too afraid to involve him in a danger that could cause him some kind of harm. He knew Sikander was itching to prove his manhood but it was his hot-headedness that scared his father. He knew this was the job of an even-tempered man, someone who could deal patiently with a disturbed and agitated victim of kidnapping, someone who could smile and chat up the patrol officers on countless checkposts, all the way from the cities to the dust bowl of Nushki.

Sikander was nothing like that. One small mistake could give them away, put their location on the map and expose their secret. The truth was, Rustom believed he could never trust Sikander with his profession. What he did was a highly volatile job, for he never knew the identity of the people who gave him the assignments. No one came to visit the victims and he was solely responsible for them unless the assignees received their ransom and finally asked him to let go of the captives. What Rustom got in return for his services to kidnap and provide food and shelter to the abductees, was just enough to suffice in the kitchenette and probably get a pair of new clothes for all of them on Eid.

Until last year, Habiba had counted that they had had 164 captives. This year was drastically different since this one was only the eighteenth person the men had brought in during the last six months. She could see that her father was more agitated than before. Less work meant little wage; he was going through a rough patch in his career. The stricter border control along the Durand Line was making his work harder. Still, he managed to keep his cool in front of the girls. He patted their heads as soon as they bent their necks in front of him to say 'Salama Lekum'. He would quietly wash his hands in the metallic basin that Habiba brought to his side as he sat on a mat with his son. And he never criticized his elder daughter Ayesha's cooking. She baked naans in the clay oven the family had dug outside their tents. The tandoor served as the only appliance in their kitchen. Sikander had grown accustomed to the seasonal birds and would hunt down a couple every day to be roasted in the tandoor, as the condiment to the basic bread. If they were lucky, Bashir would bring down a raw or cooked leg of lamb or rib rack, and that would be devoured hungrily by everyone.

That afternoon, when the new prisoner had been brought in and the men had eaten, Ayesha knew she had to cook extra for the new guest. Once she was done baking the naans for the new man, she rubbed a little congealed sheep fat atop the surface of the bread to keep it moistened.

'Sikander!' she called out to her little brother, to carry the cane-woven plate of naans, a chhabi, to the newly arrived prisoner. She had loved Sikander as her child after the death of their mother five years ago. He had been nine and wouldn't stop crying for days. Ayesha had been responsible for the family since then. She had had a hard time taming the little rebel in Habiba and kept scolding her for wandering too far during her walks around the mountain or going too near the wall of purdah. Ayesha was kept on her toes most of the time by all the family members. She also knew

## Habiba

she had turned old enough to field the question about marriage.

Ayesha had not yet had any exposure to men in her seventeen-year-old life, except her father and brother. Bashir was the only other person who was allowed to roam around their tents when he came to check on the abductees. He was responsible for unlocking their chains and allowing them to walk for a couple of hours every day. Sometimes, if there was a group of people, Bashir insisted on playing cricket with them and Sikander. He would bring a worn-out bat and a hollowed ball wrapped with duct tape, and a makeshift team would take turns to bowl, bat and field. Bashir ate with them, and finally, after it was made sure that all of them had had their turns to eat, they would work out, go to the toilet and bathe (an old, two-litre oil canister filled with water was the daily ration per person), after which they were all again securely fastened to their chains and then Bashir would leave. Ayesha had often seen Bashir stealing glances across the compound when she would peep out of the tent to bring the sleeping mats inside or to hang her washed linen on the rocky wall next to her abode. At first, she thought he, too, was doing his job of protecting the family's honour by keeping an eye on the women. But after some time, it seemed a little too much to her.

She knew Sikander disliked him for being too close to his father but Ayesha also felt uncomfortable when he was around. Habiba was not very careful in her step and she would also go to say 'salam' to Bashir if their paths crossed. If Habiba spotted him looking in her direction as she stepped out of the tent to go heat up the tandoor for Ayesha, she would wave at him and he would just stare back. Sometimes, he smiled. To the younger girl, he was like a family member, but Ayesha wasn't convinced. She considered him to be an intruder.

'You are just too doubtful of everything,' Habiba would say, shaking her head. Ayesha didn't argue but she couldn't shun the thoughts of Bashir keeping an eye on her, in particular.

That evening, Bashir did not come back to eat or play with the kidnapped man. Rustom had ordered to keep him hungry for the rest of the day so he would be manageable. The father and son sat quietly beside a small bonfire as the sun started to dim. The girls went inside their tent, took off their heavy headgear and sighed in relief. Now there would be no interference in their tranquil life. Habiba helped Ayesha to undo her twelve braids that kept her long, flowy hair in place inside the chador, the mirrored hat and the scarf that kept the rest of the headgear in place. As she untwisted the bronze hair of her sister, she could smell a mixture of perspiration and coriander oil. Ayesha ran her hands over the strands of her hair in relief, combed them with her fingers and let them loose around her shoulders in a way that the tips of her hair touched the ground. Habiba admired her sister's beauty. She herself was no less than a gem in the wild, but her sister was equally striking. She had hazel-coloured eyes and a pouted set of lips. Her nose was small and buttonish, which made her look like a porcelain doll. Ayesha was exactly what her name meant—dazzling.

She was at that juncture in her life where she knew she would be wedded off soon. To whom, she had no idea, but she had dreams. She fantasized about living in a brick house. She did not imagine curtains of silk and sofas upholstered in brocade, but she certainly wanted a room with walls for herself; a room that wouldn't blow off with a dust storm, or soak when it poured once a year. She blushed in solitude when she thought of a man of her own, with whom she could shamelessly share a room. She felt her cheeks burn when she thought of sleeping close to a man, without anyone else in sight. To her surprise, when she tried to imagine a faceless man in her daydreams, the bearded face of Bashir popped up in her brain. She would shudder from head to toe. Sometimes she would sit up, alarmed at the tricks her brain played on her. She would wipe beads of sweat from her brow, drink a handful of water from the clay pot near her bed at Habiba's feet, and wipe her face with her wet hands. She would then slap her head for being so nasty.

The girl wasn't aware that it was her heart that was playing games with her head, and not the other way around. That night, when Habiba slowly rubbed her sister's scalp with jasmine oil to refresh her, Ayesha was thinking about Bashir. Earlier in the afternoon, as he was about to drive off in his jeep, their eyes had briefly met and he had looked away. Ayesha noticed he never stared at their tent when Rustom was around. Habiba, the more brazen one had said 'salam' to him after greeting her father and frowning at her brother. Puzzled, he had glanced towards Rustom, who was as stony-faced as ever. He briefly said 'walekum salam' and paced towards his jeep. Ayesha began to wonder why he never spoke to her and instead preferred glancing.

A young girl's heart is a very vulnerable place. It is capable of housing several feelings at the same time. Fear, excitement, shame, love, passion, awe, guilt, responsibility, liberation, restlessness—all of these can be felt by her at a singular moment when she discovers she is in love. At that instant, when Habiba had combed her sister's hair and had sat in front of Ayesha so she could return the favour by combing hers, Ayesha realized why her heart beat faster when she laid eyes on Bashir. She felt the air leave her lungs for a moment because all her life, she had been burdened with the responsibility of considering herself no more than a liability. She had been conditioned to think of herself as the yoke on her father's shoulders that had to be removed some day.

As she ran her fingers across Habiba's dark hair to untangle the tresses, Ayesha felt ashamed. She was committing a sin by thinking of Bashir in that particular way. She was being disloyal to her father by letting herself imagine the unimaginable. She tried to shun the thoughts by shaking her head but her heart was in no mood to relent. Why, she asked herself, would her father allow Bashir to come regularly to the house? They had never seen any male cousin of theirs. Rustom did not take them down to the town for any occasion, be it a wedding, the annual feast or the two Eids.

Maybe Sikander had a whiff of what Rustom had planned, thought Ayesha, engaged in a verbal duel with her heart and mind. Maybe Rustom had, after all, planned to place Bashir in charge of his work and to make him part of the family. This last assumption brought a shy smile to her lips.

'Ow!' Habiba exclaimed, and brought her sister back to the real world. She had, in her racing train of thoughts, accidentally pulled a strand of her sister's hair.

'Wabakhai (Sorry),' Ayesha apologized with a smile.

'Khodai de wabakha (Only God can forgive you).' Habiba pulled a face.

Ayesha laughed and grasped her little sister in both her arms, brought her close for a hug and they both tickled and wrestled playfully as Habiba laughed and struggled to free herself from her sister's hold. Ayesha kissed her on the cheek and told her to kiss her back.

'Za! (Go away!)' said Habiba, finally managing to escape. She wriggled into her camp bed and wrapped the thick bedcover over her head. Ayesha did the same, but with a smile on her face. Both of them lay awake in their beds. The night was still young.

'Do you remember mother sharing this tent with us?' Habiba asked her sister.

Ayesha turned towards her sister and said, 'I remember everything.'

'I wish she was alive,' said Habiba, filling the atmosphere with a wistful sadness.

For once, Ayesha, the motherly one, didn't have anything to say. She wished the same, too, but it was a desire beyond hope. Both of them went quiet and wrapped their blankets tighter around themselves as the chill of the night crept inside their tent and the ground became colder.

During some part of the night, Habiba woke up to the sound of Sikander hissing abuse in Pushto. She looked at Ayesha, who was enveloped in her blanket. Habiba got out of her bed and peeped through the tent to see Sikander standing near the wall of purdah, whispering curses to the new prisoner. Habiba couldn't understand what the tanned man was saying but the angry abuse of her brother made her comprehend the situation a little—the chill of the night had probably forced the prisoner to ask for a blanket, and Sikander, the tough night-guard, had turned the request down. She felt ashamed of her brother—a Pukhtoon who could not treat his guests right. She walked out with her blanket. Sikander was still spitting insults. She patted him on the shoulder and he turned around, startled.

'What are you doing here?' he almost barked.

'Give him the blanket. It is cold out here.' She wasn't bothered by his tone.

'You have no business coming in here,' he hissed angrily to his sister and looked at the prisoner who was staring at both of them.

'What are you looking at?' he yelled at the prisoner and ran towards him to threaten him. Habiba saw her brother go closer to the frightened man and hit his back with the butt of his Kalashnikov.

'What is wrong with you?' Habiba complained loud enough to wake her father and sister. She had unknowingly crossed the wall of purdah and was standing in the prisoners' compound. She had had enough of her brother's domineering personality, and did not see the rest of her family members come behind her. Emboldened by the high moral-cultural ground he suddenly found himself standing on, he took a fistful of his sister's hair and pushed her backwards. She cringed in pain but her brother kept tugging at her hair.

# Habiba

'Sikander,' Rustom's commanding voice boomed through the sheer silence of the night.

Both of them froze. Ayesha was already a gaping statue, standing at the threshold of her tent.

'You cannot dishonour your sister!' Rustom's voice was gruff.

'She is strutting around shamelessly with her hair open, offering her blanket to the stranger!' Sikander made it sound like a capital sin.

Rustom put up one hand to silence him. He looked at Habiba who was standing with her head hanging. She wasn't sure what her father would do or say. Rustom simply told her to go to bed.

'And don't offer your bedding to a man other than your husband,' he said through gritted teeth. Habiba trembled a little and ran back to her asylum. Ayesha quickly joined her and they threw down the drapes of the tent as if they would be invisible behind them.

'Sikander, go give the prisoner your bedding.'

Sikander wore a scowl on his face. His face twitched in agitation and as he opened his mouth to say something, Rustom ordered him to do as told. Clenching his teeth, the fourteen-year-old boy grabbed the bedding from in front of the bonfire and threw it on the prisoner's face. He stormed back to his position of night-guard and Rustom went back to his tent.

Daybreak was just a couple of hours away.

Before the first ray of the sun reached the earth, the muezzin called out for prayer and that is when the tranquil silence of the plateau changed into a humming buzz. Everyone, including the prisoner, had performed their ablutions. The men said their prayers together and the two girls did it in solitude in their tent. Sikander then ran up and down the mountain. He would keep his routine up, to and fro, until the strength in his tendons had been tested enough. He wanted to convince his father that he was strong and man enough to take on an assignment with him. Bashir had become an eyesore to him.

About a fortnight since the last prisoner had been taken by Rustom, he received a new assignment. The man had to be picked from Abottabad, a close-by city known for its natural beauty. Rustom briefly told his son about the assignment, and allotted the night-guard to him, although it was not his turn. Rustom needed a good night's sleep for the next day's excursion.

Sikander was visibly disturbed. He hated the sight of everything—the bonfire, the prisoner's tent in front of him, the prisoner inside it. His inner commotion made him take a sudden decision. He abandoned his post, walked down the Jamaldini road that led to the village around twelve miles down and awoke Bashir.

'Baba says we have to go urgently,' he lied to his older cousin. He needed Bashir, for someone had to drive the jeep, and one of them should know the whereabouts of the new 'assignment'. Bashir, befuddled, trusted his cousin and they both went off in the silence of the night.

It was not until the prayer call that Rustom realized his son was missing. The girls were puzzled and worried; the father was perplexed. They first waited for some time, thinking he would

## Habiba

return from his exercise. At daybreak, Rustom followed the same trail his son had taken the previous night and took off in his search for Bashir. Upon reaching, he was told by Bashir's family that he had gone to work with Sikander. Rustom slapped his forehead with his hand and cursed a little.

'The boy knows nothing,' he was muttering to himself. 'He will get me caught; compromise my hideout. That idiot, oxen-headed clown! How will he answer the questions of the patrol people? What shall he say to them?'

Rustom was leaping up the steep road that would take him back to the girls. He had to leave them alone for the day and follow the boys to Abbottabad. The easiest way for a safe transport was to shroud the kidnapped person in a burka and put him on the back seat with Bashir. When someone asked, they would say it's a newly wed couple and Rustom is the driver. The licence, too, was in Bashir's name, so all would be foolproof.

What Rustom feared the most was how they would justify themselves. What if the prisoner took them for a couple of harmless boys, and jumped or made sounds in front of the policemen? Rustom shuddered at the thought. He reached home, told the girls that they were on their own for the day and headed towards the nearest bus stop from where he could reach Abbottabad. Bashir had all the details of the abductee but Rustom had never allowed him to do the job alone.

With the men gone, the girls huddled in their tent and waited until someone would arrive. After a couple of hours until Habiba spoke up, 'Ayesha, I am hungry.' Ayesha knew it was almost midday and they could not spend the entire day inside the tent without food and water. So she went out, lit the tandoor and got ready to bake the naans. Fresh dough was kneaded and rolled out into beautifully rounded circles to be stuck on the walls of the tandoor and eaten along with tea or qehwa. Just as they had cooked their share of bread, Habiba remembered they had company.

'He is hungry, too,' she said, pointing towards the guest on the other side of the wall of purdah. Ayesha rolled her eyes. 'Have you lost your mind? Have you forgotten what happened that night?'

'What? That? That was Sikander gone crazy.'

'I will not let you go near the wall, do you hear that?' Ayesha warned her, hitting her sister's hand with the long pair of tongs she held to remove the naan from the smoking tandoor.

'If you are lazy to not cook for him, I will give him my share.' Habiba had the stubborn streak like Sikander, and stood up with her breakfast.

Ayesha, the motherly one, gave up reasoning with her sister at the prospect of her going hungry.

'Okay, sit down and eat. I will cook more for him,' she said helplessly.

Habiba sat down with a smug smile and began eating. Ayesha rolled her eyes at her.

By the time the guest's breakfast was ready, Habiba had gobbled down half her bread and all her qehwa.

'Now, do what you want but be careful and don't go too close.' Ayesha handed her sister the food.

## Habiba

'Will he bite me?' Habiba asked playfully.

'This is no joke, Habiba. If someone sees you, they will chop off our noses.'

Habiba pulled a face of disbelief and fixed her veil on her face in a way that only her topaz-coloured eyes were visible. She walked gingerly towards the wall, took a deep breath upon reaching there, looked back at her sister who was watching her like a hawk and then kept approaching the guest's tent.

'Food?'

She didn't know what to say to the prisoner who was lying inside the tent, his torso covered and his legs out in the open. He sat up when he heard the voice and looked out. He was awed to see the same girl standing outside his tent. The last time she had come this close, he had to take the blow of the Kalashnikov's butt from her brother. He quickly extended his hand when he saw the food. Habiba complied and handed him over the bread. She was about to turn back when she saw that his ankles were bleeding and the wounds were gathering pus. She cringed a little but the prisoner could not see the alteration in her facial expression, not only because she was covered in a veil but also because he was eating hungrily like a famished dog.

Habiba returned to her sister who heaved a sigh of exasperation and began clearing the hearth. Habiba disappeared into the tent and came out with a jar of herbal medicine.

'What is this now?' Ayesha asked, alarmed.

'Shhh... it will take a moment,' Habiba said, and ran towards the forbidden patch of land. She went towards the prisoner and he looked at her quizzically. She extended her hand and offered him the medicine. He didn't quite understand and questioned with his hands.

Habiba bent and pointed towards the wounds and pus and made rubbing signs in the air.

'Oh,' the man said, 'thank you.'

Habiba was about to turn back when she felt the ground beneath her feet tremble a little. The faint trembling turned into a buzz within a second and she saw Bashir's jeep approach the land. Blood drained from her face and all she could think of doing was to take refuge in the prisoner's tent. She hid there as quickly as possible and left the man with his mouth hanging open.

The jeep parked near the stove where Ayesha sat quivering in fear. Bashir and Sikander had returned empty-handed because they had been late to execute the plan. They were supposed to kidnap the 'assignment' during his commute from home to office but they had missed him. The plot had been delayed till the next day and Sikander wore a dismal expression on his face. He had failed in his attempt at proving something that was so important to his ego and manhood. He knew he had gone ten steps backward with this failure. He angrily scowled at Ayesha whose throat was laden with thorns. She didn't even notice Bashir staring at her.

'Where's Baba?' he asked her and she mumbled with much difficulty that he had gone after them.

Bashir took off his Pukhtoon cap from his head and threw it on the ground.

## Habiba

'This boy...this foolish boy has cost me my dignity before Rustom,' he muttered to himself, looking at Sikander. He sat in the jeep and rode back towards the village.

The 'foolish boy' could not bear his family members looking at his face full of failure, so he turned to the prisoner and to make him his whipping boy.

'Who gave you this?' he thundered, when he saw the half-eaten naan in his hands. He awaited a reply from the terrified prisoner, who had had nothing to do with the arrival of the breakfast. He didn't know what to say and as Sikander's eyes searched him, he spotted the bottle of herbal medicine.

'What is going on here?' he stormed. He punched the prisoner's face and shouted at Ayesha.

'Where is Habiba?'

Ayesha's heart sank a million fathoms in that second. Her mouth went dry and her face went pale.

'Where is she?' Sikander grabbed his sister's hair through the chador she wore and shook her vehemently. Habiba was as frightened as one would be at the threshold of the hanging rope. She could not show face. Sikander stopped looking for answers and started searching for his sister. He looked into his own tent, his sisters' tent and stood frozen on the ground, his fists clenched, his head tilted upwards and his body as stiff as steel.

He looked at Ayesha, his eyes blazing, his mouth foaming, and said, 'By Allah, if she is found where I am now going to look, I shall not spare her.'

Having said that, he marched towards the prisoner's tent, kicked the man on his way and walked in. His face turned red and his mouth spat a spurt of abuses at his sister. She pleaded it was not what he thought but Sikander would not wait a second more.

'I have sworn to Allah,' was the last thing he said to his sister before angling the Kalashnikov on his shoulder and aiming for her head.

The only thing Sikander got right that day, was his aim. Habiba, squatting on the ground, received a bullet between her eyes, exactly where she would have worn a coin of gold when she would have dressed up as a bride. Her topaz eyes were wide open and the rest of her was covered in black. She fell backward as she got hit. Ayesha put her hands on her mouth and screamed. Sikander wasn't quite done yet. He pulled the trigger once again and shot the 'accomplice' in Habiba's crime. With both of them dead, Sikander slung his weapon back on his shoulder and walked towards Ayesha.

'Where is father?'

Ayesha was sitting on the ground, in the same posture as a few seconds ago. She was in a stupor. Sikander cruelly shook her by the shoulder but she was as stiff as Habiba's dead body. The brother, with his honour intact, went inside his tent.

Rustom returned home at dusk. He brought Bashir along with him. As he stepped down from the jeep, he saw Ayesha sleeping on the ground near the stove. It was strange, for the women never slept out in the open. Sikander had crept out of his abode when he heard the hum of the jeep.

'What happened to Ayesha?' Rustom asked. He was feeling rather embarrassed that his elder daughter was sleeping in the courtyard with Bashir to witness. Bashir, however, was looking away. He had been reprimanded by Rustom for listening to Sikander and as Rustom gave his son his share of the chide, Bashir walked towards the prisoner to give him his daily dose of exercise at dusk. The scene he saw there, left him speechless.

He cried out in pain. Rustom ran to see what had made Bashir scream and he, too, could not believe his eyes. Habiba, which meant 'the dearest', and who had been named by her father himself, was lying as lifelessly as a rag doll. He removed her veil to confirm that it was her. Her open mouth, which had begun to sag, established that it was indeed her.

Sikander came behind him and told his father he had 'found' them together. Rustom's eyes shot up, as did Bashir's, but no one asked any questions.

It was a matter of honour.

Rustom sprinkled water on Ayesha' face and rubbed her feet. When she opened her eyes, she ran to the wall of purdah and crossed it without thinking. She saw her sister's body and wept like a mad woman. Her cries didn't subside even when dusk changed to night and night changed to day.

At dawn, Rustom and Sikander buried the man after giving him his final bath. Ayesha did it for her sister. Bashir was the only attendee in the janazah, the funeral prayer. As soon as it was over, Ayesha looked ten years older and chronically sick. Rustom had decided something for his daughter. He took Bashir inside his tent, leaving Ayesha to hug her sister's grave. Moments later, when the men came out, Bashir went towards his own house down the dwindling road and Rustom came closer to Ayesha.

'Bashir will wed you this Friday,' he told her. Ayesha did not have the energy to say or feel anything. Happiness was a word she couldn't recognise any more. She only wept as she sat beside Habiba in her grave.

Despite her loss, Ayesha got her dream fulfilled. Bashir and his family came for a solemn nikah. They gave her some trousseau and ate Rustom's food merrily, after which they took the bride home. Ayesha got a room with four walls and a door for herself and Bashir. Her in-laws had brought her a bridal outfit and she indeed looked dazzling as a bride. Her eyes were puffy from the crying and her pouty mouth more swollen than before. The famine of the past week had highlighted her cheekbones to a sharp angle and with such natural beauty, she did not need cosmetics at all. Other than the stone jewellery her father gave her, she also wore a string of beads around her neck. It had belonged to Habiba.

Her eyes had welled up several times during her wedding, thinking of her baby sister. The only way she could feel her presence was through the beads she wore. When it was time for the baaraat to leave with the bride, Rustom placed his hand on her head, stiff-faced as ever, and Sikander was nowhere to be seen. Maybe he did not care or maybe he was too proud to let anyone see him cry. That, too, shall remain a mystery. Anyhow, once in her husband's house, Ayesha was led into her own private asylum. The family elders sent Bashir in to consummate his marriage as per tradition.

Afterwards, Ayesha dared to think for a moment, that with Habiba gone, she was left with only Bashir to love. Rustom and

## Habiba

Sikander could take care of themselves. She even smiled when, later in the night, she saw Bashir sleeping beside her. The next day, Bashir had gone off to see Rustom to talk about work, and Ayesha started tidying up the room she had a claim to. She smiled, completely in love with the man who had taken her the night before. She belonged to him fully—mind, heart, body and soul. In her excursions through the eight-by-eight-feet room, she found a small box hidden under a heap of crumpled clothes. She opened it to find a woman's ring—steel, thus not very expensive, but studded with a big topaz. She was not educated enough to know the name of the semi-precious stone, but it reminded her of something close to her heart. It looked so familiar.

She thought hard but she was unable to hear what the stone screamed out at her. She put it back, thinking it must belong to Bashir's mother or sister. Her days were spent more delightfully than before, for the little girls in Bashir's clan were sent to school. They loved Ayesha, the new paternal aunt, or 'mumani' as they called her, and sat with her after lessons, teaching her what they learnt at school. She also stitched dresses for them or their dolls. She found friends in her in-laws and although she wept in silence when she thought of her sister, she knew Bashir had slowly taken up most of her love.

A few weeks later, Bashir gave her the ring to wear.

'Is it for me?' she had asked, surprised.

'I bought it for the girl I would marry...' he said quietly, and paused.

'So yes, it's for you,' he added.

Ayesha happily wore it on her finger and as soon as she did, an image flashed across her eyes. Habiba. Her eyes. Topaz was the colour of her sister's eyes.

When she came out of that stupor, she rationalized. If Bashir had bought it for the girl he planned on marrying... she couldn't think more.

She glanced at Bashir who had lied down on the bed and had put one arm on her waist, closing his eyes like a satisfied man. She told the flush on her face to recede, for she had nothing to complain about. She returned her husband's embrace and closed her eyes to sleep.

# Nazia
*In pursuit of happiness*

Imran had been checking out his reflection in the glass pane of his classroom's window. Although he had been quite sure of his debonair demeanour when he had left for the school that morning, he still wanted to make sure that the tedious routine of the school day had not dulled the brightness of his form. He straightened out the creases of his electric blue shirt and readjusted the silvery grey tie. He glanced down to see his favourite faded blue jeans making his legs look as shapely as possible. He was very proud of the 'branded' sneakers and wristwatch that he had bought off a street vendor at a cheap price. Pleased with his appearance, he smiled smugly. Once again, he looked through the window and saw a stampede of school boys, pushing, nudging, teasing and racing with each other in a bid to reach the gate earlier.

Imran, too, was feeling as impatient as the boys at that

moment because he needed Nazia to see him when he had preened himself to the fullest. He had never been this conscious about himself. He wanted to look his best since she always looked effortlessly beautiful in those flowy kurtas and chooridaars. It had never occurred to him that she could be the mother of one child. His heart had sunk when she had brought her son, Mustapha, to the annual staff dinner at the school, but he had learnt by the end of the night that she was a divorcee. That had sparked a warm light of hope in his heart. At present, he could feel the same warmth in his face, when he saw Nazia also looking out for him through her classroom's window.

Imran's heart jumped to his mouth for a brief second when she sent him an acknowledging smile, but they were both careful to not wave or signal anything, lest a pupil or colleague should spot them. That could get ugly on many levels. They both, however careful, could not bar the rosy glow of love shining in full glory on their faces as their eyes met. While Imran had taken his time to look presentable to his lady-love, Nazia had hardly found time to dust off the chalk residue from her hair. When her eyes had met with Imran's, she had briefly smiled before quickly lowering her eyes.

Whatever was blossoming between her and her colleague at the primary school for boys, was something new to her. She had reluctantly thought of the word 'love', had shuddered and let the thought slip away. It scared her a little. She was not sure what Imran's intentions were... was he being friendly just to the point where he could pull away when it would be time to commit, or was he interested enough to become a father to her son? It was thoughts like the former that made her keep her distance from Imran, even though, she had to admit, she enjoyed his company and the long conversations with him on the phone.

Awaiting a radio silence to prevail in the school campus, Nazia had cleaned the chalkboard, muttering under her breath about when the promised whiteboards would make it to the classrooms. She was a History teacher and, for that, she usually had to vehemently use the blackboard to make maps, charts and graphs. Later, she sat down with the huge pile of notebooks the students had left on their desks. Imran and she had this worked out—they would mark the notebooks together every weekend and if someone objected, they could always play the 'colleague' card, saying Nazia needed help from Imran Sir, the Geography teacher, regarding a History lesson. A divorced woman can never be too careful, especially when people around are looking for reasons to blame her for not being able to work out a marriage.

When she reached the fourth notebook to check the answers to a pop quiz regarding Chandragupta and Ashoka's era in the subcontinent, she heard a soft tap on the door. It was a natural reflex action for her eyes to pull their gaze away from the scribbled handwriting of a ten-year-old and move it towards the door, and with the same impulse, her hand reached out to fix her dupatta over her fully-rounded bosom.

'Hello!' Imran had hoped to sound as charming as Lionel Richie. The smile on Nazia's face assured him that his appearance had taken her attention.

'You look good,' he said, as he pulled a chair to sit beside her. She glanced down at her clothes and knew she had spent a little longer than usual in choosing her attire from the miniscule wardrobe that she owned—a dozen kurtas that were sold at half the price outside elitist boutiques in the posh localities of Lahore. The sellers were usually Pukhtoon men who had been running the roadside business in urban cities of Pakistan for decades. Their families stayed behind in the mountainous Khyber Pakhtunkhwa province, while these men earned their living selling fake designer outfits, shoes and accessories.

'Thank you, Imran,' she said briefly.

'How's Mustapha?' he said, trying to begin with small talk.

'He's good, thanks.' She always felt pleased when he asked about her son.

Nazia had stopped checking the notebooks. Imran was a talkative person and probably that was one of the prime reasons she enjoyed his company. He was so interested in talking about his opinions that she could, for a while, stop thinking about her messy past that kept lunging from the subconscious nooks of her brain to the conscious fore.

'Has Madam Rukhsana assigned you a job for the annual play?' he asked.

'Not yet, but she said she could make use of an extra pair of hands at the rehearsals. So, I do not quite know yet.' She paused, and then added, 'What about you?'

'Oh, I have no interest in all this drama-shrama, but Madam told me to become the assistant director, since Rana Saab has a problem staying back at school after closing time.' He was a little boastful, Nazia knew, but she never said so.

'So, you are going to be staying back every day?' She was

more than a little impressed, for she could never do that. Her son deserved her time and attention when she was done earning their bread and butter at 2 p.m. every afternoon.

'I guess I shall have to.' He checked the time on his watch. 'Actually, it was the fifth time he had done that ever since he came here,' Nazia thought to herself. 'He never did that before… so maybe he was getting late for something …or to be more exact, he had never worn a watch before.' 'Oh,' she thought, and almost chuckled; she finally understood that he was showing off his watch.

'That's a fine watch,' she commented, thinking that was probably what he wanted—a little appreciation from a girl he was hanging out with. It cost her nothing really…she actually felt grateful that he chose to accompany her when her girlfriends, too, had become sceptical about her.

'Oh, why, thank you!' he said, feigning surprise. 'It's a Rado,' he added, when she did not ask him what brand he wore.

She made a 'thumbs up' sign and saw him gloat a little. She laughed inwardly.

'Men!' she thought; they have an incessant need to have their ego fed. She needed to ask no second question to be assured that it was a counterfeit Rado, just like her fake designer kurta, because she had seen him wear a pair of fake branded sneakers everyday which bore a logo spelled 'ADDIDAS'.

'Why do you give them so much work?' Imran pulled a face when he saw the scores of pages she had to mark per notebook.

She smiled. 'Why, you don't?'

He stretched a little and yawned. 'No,' he said, looking at his watch again.

'Damn,' he thought, 'her conversation never goes beyond the school and students. What am I to her?' His frustration was evident on his face and he stood up as if to leave. Nazia's eyes followed his actions. 'Do you want to go to the canteen for a plate of chaat?' he asked.

Nazia was horrified at the idea. 'No, I don't think that's a very good idea, Imran,' she replied immediately.

Imran looked disappointed.

'Not even as friends?'

She looked at him and felt a sense of pity. He was a year older than her but he was single, unlike her. He must be expecting a giggly, overly excited girlfriend, which she wasn't. She could not just go out for a plate of chaat with him even at the canteen, for wagging tongues couldn't be stopped. She was thinking of an appropriate reply to his question with her head hung and her chin over her breast, while Imran was eyeing up the girl of his interest. She had a full bosom but a small waist. No one would ever think that she had had a baby. Her legs were shapely and her face was oval. What was most striking to him, were the small beads of perspiration on her neck that slowly slid down the arch and got lost upon entering the neckline of her pale yellow kurta.

Imran was still lost in his thoughts, imagining the new destination of the droplets, when Nazia looked up and saw him staring at her neckline. Imran came out of his trance when she fixed her dupatta firmly on her shoulders and let its width drop to her waist.

'I am getting late,' she said rather curtly and got up.

'So, next Saturday?' he asked, embarrassed at being caught ogling.

'Maybe, if I am not busy with the play,' she had suddenly lost interest in talking to him any more.

Both of them disappointed, they parted ways. At the gate of the school, she wanted to call out for a rickshaw since her legs and feet hurt with all the day's work, and the load of notebooks she carried was too much to manage in a bus full of sweaty people. But the luxury of a rickshaw was not something she could afford at liberty. She stopped for a moment and thrust her hand into the bag slung over her shoulder. She fumbled for currency notes and as she felt the coarse texture of roughened paper on her hands, she pulled out the folded money and saw what she had on her—two hundred-rupee notes and a twenty rupee note. She would have to pay eighty rupees for a private ride home on a rickshaw, with her pile of notebooks sitting comfortably beside her on the faux leather seat. The vision seemed good, but then the innocent face of her three-year-old son, who had been asking for a pizza for the past few days, flashed across her mind; she had been feeding him a triangle-shaped omelette instead. Her payday was still three days away but she had promised Mustapha a small six-inch pizza for dinner tonight. She needed two hundred rupees and her luxurious ride would make her break the promise—again.

Nazia shunned the thoughts of the rickshaw and decided to walk down to the bus stop and wait for the local transport. It would cost her ten rupees. That much she could afford. On the bus, she could not find space to sit so she went to the corner of the ladies' section, placed her notebooks on the floor and stood beside them, supporting the stack of books with her shins so they wouldn't scatter onto the feet of other passengers. Her kurta was drenched in perspiration and so was her face. The humid summer of Lahore becomes worse when the odour of sweat, cheap perfume, talcum powder and washing powder mix with the meagre amount of oxygen in the compressed ladies' compartment of the local bus.

Supporting her frail self in the bus, she looked out of the tinted windows and thought of the similarities between her bus ride and the roller coaster that life had been for her since a young age.

She had been a student of Urdu literature all her life. Poetry and drama had been the air she breathed for all her college years. Nazia had gone through the passage of rites like most girls in Lahore—she had been pushed by her parents to score well in the exams every year and had been encouraged to dream big for herself. Like most girls who had been born and bred in middle-class families, she, too, had dreamed of a career. She desired to be a poetess or scriptwriter like the celebrated women writers who had carved a niche for themselves in Urdu literature.

However, when she had finished her Master's degree and had plans to write a book of poetry while pursuing her dream of research with an MPhil degree, she had been shoved into the abyss of marriage, becoming just another prospective bride waiting to be chosen. It was a known fact that during the hunt for a groom, it is not the girl who gets to choose the boy. Rather,

*Nazia*

*she* gets chosen and is expected to go with the flow. Nazia, too, had been dolled up several times to appear before many men who were looking for a suitable girl. She was taught about the right rituals so many times by her mother that she had started to feel fed up with the whole process.

'Yes, Ammi, I will not smile.'

'Alright, I will not look into the boy's eyes.'

'Okay, I will respond to every question with a smile.'

'How on earth can I *pretend* to be shy?'

'But I don't want to wear a burka like the women in his family do.'

'Alright, I will sit with my head bent.'

She felt like an animal trainer's pet monkey, whose every gesture was being monitored and controlled. After a dozen such episodes, she was finally chosen by a family. Once the girl's beauty and education were approved of, the families took a long time and several meetings to establish their financial backgrounds, their social standing, the roots they had had in the subcontinent, the sectarian differences between the families and the dowry issues.

Nazia had had an arranged marriage. She got all the pomp of a wedding that her father could afford. Later in the night, the first time she was alone with her husband, was when she had to let him consummate their marriage. She had thought about it a lot, all day, and had no clue how to respond to the man she hardly knew or had spoken to not more than once. She understood the man would be rightfully doing his duty in taking her to be his own. However, if a carnal connection was the first step to building the most fragile relationship in her life, she was quite unimpressed with the whole idea of marriage.

The bus driver's voice boomed through the radio transmitters. She had reached her destination. She had a couple of minutes before the automatic door on the metro bus closed and that was ample time for her to collect all her stuff. The walk down to her house was a little less than a kilometre. She was attentive to the smallest detail of how well her dupatta was perched atop her shoulders, covering her upper body and her hair as well. Every time the dupatta slipped, she tugged at it as if her life depended on it.

It took her around twenty minutes to reach the threshold of her doorstep from the bus stop. That afternoon, the sun was hazy, and the scorching heat and humid air were killing animals and humans alike. As she thought of Imran, the school play and Mustapha, in different but knotted strings of thoughts, she felt someone squeeze her bottom. Bewildered, she turned back to see what had just happened, when a blurry but huge hand flicked some cigarette ash into her eyes. She could hear hyena-like, muffled laughs coming from around her. The ash in her eyes had made her drop the notebooks and she could not really perceive the scene in front of her. She was rubbing her eyes and water poured copiously from them. She wasn't even sure whether it was the self-cleansing system of the eyes or whether she was crying out of sheer agitation, frustration and anger. She could barely keep her eyes open when she saw the blurry form of two teenage boys—boys the age of her students—laughing and enjoying their 'manly' moment. She wanted to run after them and slap them both silly, but her brave idea was interrupted by the putt-putting of a scooter that had halted right beside her.

'Is something wrong?' the rider asked her. She was in a mood to punch just about anybody and the sympathy from a stranger, sincere or not, blew the whistle off her head, which was already boiling like a pressure cooker. She let out a stream of abuse at him. He didn't answer back, readjusted the gear and rode away. She was still screaming in the middle of the road, calling out names to men in general—abuse to her ex-husband and filthy names to the Pakistani society that failed to give respect to women.

She reached home in a wild state, her eyes ablaze and swollen from crying and the cigarette ash. Her notebooks were in a state of disarray. She was trying to get them to stay in a stack by balancing them on both her arms but could hardly do so. Nazia rang the doorbell and silently wished her younger sister would not answer it.

It had been an unfortunate afternoon when everything was going so wrong, and as expected, that streak of ill-fate continued with Yasmin, her younger sister, opening the door for her, wearing a scowl. She saw Nazia's red face but chose to ignore it. After opening the door, she immediately turned and walked away, leaving Nazia to deal with her demons alone. She silently shut the door behind her and followed her sister into the living room. Her mother was sitting on the sofa, shelling peas with a lady from the neighbourhood. That was her mother's ritual. If she didn't have a neighbourhood friend over for gossip, she herself would be visiting someone.

'Salama Lekum.' Nazia managed to stretch her lips into a smile for both the ladies as they stopped their chore to speak to her.

'Walaikum Salam,' they both replied in unison. Although neither bothered to make further conversation, Nazia knew what was to follow, so she rushed into her room, hoping Mustapha would be sleeping so she, too, could have some peace. It was a small house with two rooms—one belonged to the parents and the other one had always belonged to Yasmin and Nazia. Now, when she was back in her parents' house with a child, Mustapha, too, shared the sanctity of the sisters' room and that was quite annoying to Yasmin.

'What happened to her?' she heard the neighbour asking her mother.

'Who knows? This is an everyday drama,' her mother said callously.

Nazia's heart broke. She knew her mother blamed her for the divorce and also worried that since she couldn't do well as a wife, people would be reluctant to ask for Yasmin's hand in marriage.

'I have told my Yasmin, that she, too, should be ready to sit at home for the rest of her life,' her mother continued wistfully, as if the sole victim of Nazia's divorce was Yasmin.

Nazia had been listening to this kind of conversation ever since she had come back to her father's house. The reason she started working was to support herself and her son financially. She had been frustrated during all those days of iddat, the hundred days of solitude that restrict a divorced Muslim woman

## Nazia

from showing face to anyone but her blood kin. Her mother had been weeping, for the legacy of her generations had been marred. There had been no divorced woman in her family tree.

'We were taught to be flexible,' she always said, just like she was saying to her neighbour at that time, while shelling peas. Nazia hated it even more when her mother suddenly raised her voice while making such statements. She had seen Mustapha lying down near the bed, fast asleep, and didn't bother to wake him up. That would mean a whole new set of activities. So she slumped on the floor in the room, rested her head on her palms and closed her eyes.

'If you allow me to say, sister, you should marry off Yasmin when you get the first chance,' the neighbour piped in. 'And you shouldn't tell the interested parties about Nazia's failed marriage, for that would jinx the entire thing,' she added hastily.

Nazia heard her mother grunt her approval. It had been a long day for her. She had taken enough ridiculousness from her ex and the men around her, who had their eyes on her body even at those times when she didn't notice. She had listened to people blaming her for the failure of her marriage, and she had swallowed it every time. But that day she couldn't.

She left her room and strode towards the lounge where the old ladies were watching reruns of *Kyunki Saas Bhi Kabhi Bahu Thi*, and spoke in the loudest voice that she could.

'Aunty,' she addressed the neighbour, 'What failed was neither my marriage nor I. What failed was that bastard who was the poorest excuse for a husband.'

Her eyes were ablaze. The women had stopped shelling peas

and were staring at her in bewilderment. Nazia, however, was not quite done yet. She continued.

'Have you been shoved into a cupboard and gotten punched continuously by a man twice your size, for staying asleep past his breakfast time? Or, tell me, have you been pushed so hard that you have fallen flat on your face, with a man standing on your buttocks, so you don't move while he whips you with a belt, only because you don't make a perfect, round roti for his mother? HAVE YOU?' She was screaming by the time she had reached the rhetorical question that ended her speech.

'Taubah taubah!' exclaimed the neighbour, as she got up from her seat and took leave, saying, 'Thanks to the almighty, He didn't give me daughters like this! What people say is correct—100 per cent correct—that she is a blot on the family name.' She left the house while Nazia's mother was apologizing softly, pulling her by the hand to sit down. But the neighbour was doing what an abusive person does when they run out of logic and reason—she was moralizing.

Nazia did not want to fend off the daggers her mother's eyes were throwing at her, so she went back to her room. Mustapha had woken up from her yells and needed attention. She went to pick him up and made sit him on her lap. He was three and she had recently switched his milk intake from mother's milk to the formula. Still, he patted her chest, asking for milk when he was disturbed. Despite all the agitation she had experienced, she couldn't help but smile at his innocent demand. She kissed him and let him have a go, especially when it meant she could get fifteen minutes of peace, quiet and solitude while her son suckled.

## Nazia

Nazia had no idea when she had sailed into the silent abyss of sleep. When she woke up, Yasmin had turned on all the lights of the room, and was opening and closing the drawers of the dresser for no apparent reason.

'Good, you are up,' she said, addressing her older sister. 'Papa is asking for you,' she said briefly and sat on the bed, waiting for Nazia to leave.

'Ok,' she said. She gently slid the sleeping Mustapha off her arm, covered her torso with the kurta she had lifted and sat up.

'Did he have anything to eat all day?' she asked Yasmin, pointing towards Mustapha.

'Don't know... I was at college. Ask Ammi,' she said.

Nazia shifted her glance to the floor. She knew a well-fed child would be active, and up on his feet.

She quietly went to see her father. Her mother was with him. She greeted him and he stood up to embrace her.

'How are you, my daughter?' he asked with so much love that her eyes moistened. She lost her voice in the lump that had formed in her throat, and just nodded with a tight-lipped smile.

'Do you remember tomorrow is Mustapha's court meeting with his father?' he spoke gently. Nazia was grateful to him for the tone, but the reminder made her cringe.

'Yes,' she lied quietly.

'Nazia, is something bothering you?' her father asked. If someone had asked her prior to the talk with her father, what she wanted the most in the world, she would have had the following answers—peace of mind, tranquillity in the heart, bliss of the soul, happiness, companionship and some love from her sister and mother. But it was only then that she had realized that she just wanted a couple of words of concern. Maybe she could have asked for all of these, but her father was the only person who took responsibility for being fooled by the appearances of a wedding party. He told her things could be better for her in the future. She did not agree with or believe his consoling words, but they were good to hear nonetheless.

'Do you want me to go with you?'

'No, Papa.' She jerked herself upright to show her father that she was strong enough to take on the task herself. 'I shall be fine,' she reassured him. He was a nearly sixty-year-old man, close to his retirement as an administrative clerk in a government office. He had enough of his own problems, and she felt, with her divorce, she had added to his worries. So, she didn't want to physically stress him out as well.

'Alright then, where is my best friend Mustapha?' asked her father, and she nodded and left to get him. She wanted him to eat, anyway. As soon as he was up, he asked for pizza. Nazia was, for once since that afternoon, happy, for being able to provide him with that.

It was no surprise that her mother stayed quiet in her father's presence. She either knitted or kept her eyes glued to the TV screen, neither interrupting the father-daughter conversation nor avoiding it. She just stayed there.

After a quiet dinner, she had brought Mustapha back to sleep in her room, but Yasmin informed her that she had an important test the next day and would have to keep the light on all night. She even 'solved' the problem by saying that Nazia could sleep in the sitting room on the 'big' couch. Nazia told her to do well in the test, picked a pillow, her cell phone and Mustapha's cotton blanket, and left the room. Mustapha played with her for a while, for the frequent naps had taken away his desire to sleep. After an hour, she managed to put him to sleep, switched on a rechargeable torch and started on the notebooks.

While going through the history of Ashoka and Chandragupta, her mind was in a whirl, thinking about Asad, her ex-husband, and Imran, her colleague. While she was frustrated at the thought of having to see Asad tomorrow, she was also very disappointed in the latter. She liked his company and the light-hearted jokes he cracked just to make her laugh, but in the past few days, he had also become very pushy about acting like a couple. She just couldn't do that.

Or maybe she didn't want to.

The phone beeped feebly. It was Imran. He had sent a joke to her. She smiled and sent him a smiling emoticon. During the next hour, when she was only halfway through the notebooks and writing the planner for the next week, she heard a click from Yasmin's room. She had turned off the lights. Nazia looked at the half load of books waiting to be marked, shifted her gaze to her son and back again to Yasmin's room. She didn't waste time thinking any more and set off to finish her work. The torch was already dimming out.

∽

Nazia and Mustapha waited on the hard wooden bench in the small garden outside the civil court. The father had permission by the court to see his son for a couple of hours within the premises of the court and Nazia was bound by law to do this duty.

She wished, the buffoon of the man that he was, Asad would understand that his son did not recognize him or make much out of the fortnightly meetings they had. To him, it was nothing but an odd ritual with a stranger, where he did not want to leave his Mama's side. Every other Sunday, she had to sit with the oaf she had divorced just because he had demanded a twice-a-month meeting with his son. Sometimes, when he criticized his son's language skills or his physical health, she told him to mind his own business. Most of the times, they both yelled at each other before returning to their respective homes. Once, the policewoman on duty had to threaten them that she would complain to the judge about their bickering in the presence of other couples.

'Behave like them,' she had yelled. Nazia had left the building while Asad was still muttering filthy abuses at her.

That day was no different. She was prepared to listen to his nonsense, but at the same time, she had prepped her son to go see an 'uncle' who would bring him presents. Truth be told, the toys and clothes Asad brought for his son at every meeting were the only possessions Mustapha had. With the meagre salary she drew from the school, her own expenses were hardly covered. So, not only Mustapha but Nazia, too, looked forward to his gifts.

Asad appeared exactly on time at the court, holding balloons and shopping bags, as if he had recently been to a toy store. She started whispering into Mustapha's ears about the uncle who had brought gifts and that he should go play with him. With his attention was diverted to the Minion-shaped balloon, she quietly slipped away and sat on the bench at the far end of the compound from where she could watch, but not interact with, the man she held responsible for her misadventures in life.

Asad had sat his son on his lap and was bribing the kid with all sorts of candies and whatnots. Nazia glanced at them every now and then, but the rest of the time she was texting Imran. He was with his family at a brunch. He told her the food was good but the company was bad. It made her laugh. She told him she was amongst undesirable company, too, but there was no food. Imran asked her where she was and she told him. He replied saying that he had to go somewhere because all the aunties were worried about the food going cold. Weekend brunches happen in every family in Pakistan. People meet up in large or small groups to eat, after spending half the day in bed. What they eat, varies—it can be naan-chholay or nihari, halwa poori or kheer, a full English breakfast or just waffles. It really depends on what a person likes, but Sunday is never complete without a hearty brunch.

Despite all this, Nazia had left the house on an empty stomach. She always felt nauseous when she had to go to the court. The building was a bitter reminder of how hard she had to fight to get a divorce from the man who treated her worse than an animal. While her religion allowed her to get separated once she had made up her mind, the law made it hard for her to get rid of the burden of a husband forever. She had had to make appearances, prove that her husband was an abuser and fight for the custody of her child for months, and even after all that toil, there she sat, in the same compound with the same man who was now holding her precious little boy in his arms.

Nazia could see that when the display of presents was over and Mustapha had got enough candies to last a week, the child had started to get restless. She stood up to get him, but Asad signalled her to give him some more time. She sat down. The phone beeped. It was Imran calling.

'Hello, Imran?' she asked in surprise. He was supposed to be stuffing his mouth with naan and parathas.

'Yaar, where in the world are you? This place is full of mommies with their babies.' He was truly lost; the voice through the receiver sounded anxious.

'What do you—where are you?' she asked in disbelief.

'At the civil court, yaar! Now tell me, where are you sitting? And is that husband there with you?'

Nazia had completely lost her voice. She was in utter disbelief. She stood from her bench and started looking around. There were young men around her, some of them with their backs turned towards her, but none of them matched the stylish looks of Imran. She was unknowingly looking for a young man in some brightly hued tee with jeans, with faux leather shoes or those fake sneakers.

Instead, the person who walked right into her face, moments later, was someone completely different. Freshly shaven, dressed in a milky-white kurta-pajama and Peshawari chappals, Imran came closer and said 'hi' to her. She was so awed at his appearance that she forgot to feign her surprise. He looked like a man, not like a desperate boy looking for appreciation. She could smell his cologne. It was cheap, one could tell from the strong stench of spirit in it, but nonetheless, she could forgive him for that.

'What are you doing here?'

'Well, I brought you food,' he said gaily.

He needed no invitation to sit and made himself comfortable on the bench behind Nazia. 'Come, sit,' he said, 'let's eat.'

Nazia sat as he opened a small plastic box and it revealed chicken-and-cheese paratha rolls.

'These were the only transportable things on the table,' he said, grinning sheepishly. She was so taken aback by the gesture that her hands trembled as she picked up her roll and saw him eat his.

'My aunt made these,' he piped, after waiting for a while for her comment.

'It's delicious,' she mumbled. She could hardly talk.

She looked up to see where Asad had reached with his meeting with Mustapha, and saw him looking straight at her. She was scared for a moment about what he might think, but then she remembered all those times when he smelled fear on her and hit her, abused her, scratched, punched and kicked her. She remembered when he had strangled her. Some might say it is important to forget such painful events, but to Nazia, the pain had become a collection of open wounds that kept her going. She drew strength from the torment of her past. She was reminded of the night when she refused to sleep with him for her pregnant body did not allow her to do so. He had abused and slapped her, and when she still did not relent, he throttled her with both his hands until she went pale in the face. That night, when he walked out of the room in anger, she had left his house. In the middle of the night, she had reached her mother's house. She had been welcomed by all her family, but her father had seen her face and neck all black-and-blue and had not been able to forgive himself since then.

Nazia, too, had not forgiven Asad and was always reminded of all the agony he had caused her. There on the bench, sitting beside Imran, when she saw him staring at her with bloodshot eyes, she let go of all fear. She did not care any more whether people would talk behind her back about having an affair with another man or sharing a paratha with him out in the open. She did not care if Asad would call her a whore (that was his pet word for her all the time she was married to him.)

She looked towards Imran, who was studying the colours on her face very attentively.

'Why do you stare at me?' she asked him between mouthfuls.

It was Imran's turn to change facial expressions.

'No…I…what do you mean?'

He was embarrassed.

'Do you find me pretty, or are you just a frustrated piece of crap like other men?'

'Well…' he paused, 'You do know I like you a lot.'

Nazia looked into his eyes. She was not a romantic teenager who could blush at such words. She was a mother of a child, who had lost faith in relationships. She saw that Asad, who till now had been making funny faces for Mustapha and tickling him to make him laugh, had suddenly lost interest in the child and was continuously staring at her.

'Come with me,' she told him, standing up. He followed. She took him to Asad, who was now trying to console the child. He saw her coming with another man and his face darkened.

'Time's up,' she declared like an officer on duty.

'I was always right about you,' he said between gritted teeth, looking at Imran but speaking to Nazia.

'Yes, keep telling yourself that, Asad. Maybe the pain of your loss will lessen that way. Now, my son needs me.' She held Mustapha's hand and hugged him tight.

She walked with Imran towards the gate of the court and upon exiting, she told him how glad she was for his company during one of the worst times of her life. Asad walked past them when they were talking and she heard him mutter 'slut' under his breath. She decided to let him be the imbecile he was.

'I am touched that you left your family brunch for this,' she said, speaking to Imran instead.

He shrugged, 'Well, to be honest, the aunties were killing me with their rishta-brigade. And also, you won't eat chaat with me, so I had to bring parathas.'

She laughed heartily.

'Thank you, Imran,' she said, though her eyes spoke louder than her mouth.

'Anything for you,' he said.

Both of them went to their homes separately—Imran on his motorbike and Nazia on the rickshaw.

Nazia thought about Imran all day. She was sure there was no such thing as love in her heart, for him, and probably neither was there any sentimental emotion in his heart. Maybe he was just being nice. Maybe he only craved companionship. Whatever it was, she was sure of one thing—he was sincere. He had asked to be friends one day ago and she had not been very kind to him. She was paying too much heed to the people who gossiped about her and most women like her.

At night, before she slept, her phone beeped. It must be Imran, she thought with a smile. She rolled Mustapha over from her arm and reached out to get her phone from under the sofa. It was Imran.

The text read, 'I love you.'

She was flattered. While she checked herself and bit her lip when a smile came to them, her heart skipped a beat. But she kept it all under control; she could not get bitten by the same snake, twice. She had to know him better before getting into anything...even a fling.

After half an hour, she replied, 'Too early for this.'

Imran, who must have been keeping his phone close by and eyeing it like a hawk, replied within the minute, 'Sorry ☹'.

She kept looking at the lit-up screen for a while and then texted back, 'But we should have chaat and samosay together every day at school.'

'You won't feel awkward?' He was visibly confused.

'Not any more. Maybe we can go watch a movie next Sunday.'

'Really? Which one?'

'Something Mustapha can watch...animation?'

'Done! Looking forward to samosay with you tomorrow.'

## Nazia

'Me too.'

'And...we will go to the court before or after the movie?'

Her eyes welled up.

'No, the meeting is fortnightly. So I will take Mustapha next to next Sunday.'

'Yeah, we will go together.'

''

''

# Saima

### *On the trail of a dead bride*

*I*nspector Saima had been sitting in the dimly lit room with the suspect in front of her. She eyed him as he shifted uncomfortably in his chair. It had become very difficult for her to judge if his fidgety behaviour was because of the fear of getting caught or the eerie atmosphere of the questioning cell. He had been mumbling something under his breath. She had paid close attention and it seemed as if he was reciting prayers of protection against the evil. She almost chuckled.

It was ironic that he should be praying against malicious forces, for she had brought him in for being a suspect in his wife's murder. Having completed with her primary observation within a minute of being introduced with the subject, she decided it was time to lay down all the cards on the table.

'What's your name?'

'Saleem.'

*Saima*

'What do you do?'

'I am a technician.'

His voice was becoming smaller with every question. Saima observed him with interest. He was her suspect, alright, but she wanted to arrive to the conclusion of him being the culprit after knowing him through his words and not through the file a rookie officer had prepared for her (the file was complete with details starting from his birth certificate to his father's death certificate).

'Where do you work?'

She kept her eyes fixated on the file in her hands so that she could match his answers with the details contained within it.

'It's a software company, Sir—Goraya Software.'

She looked up at him. He was pale. His moustache was droopy and he did not quite look like the man on his national identity card. He looked older and also, maybe like a man in mourning. He had, to be fair, lost his wife. Even if it was an act he was pulling, she shouldn't let his outer appearance fool her into not questioning him about the intricate details of the murder.

'When did you get married to Azra?'

He paused to think, looked past her and after a few seconds, said, 'Last week, on 3rd July.'

'Right.'

His answers had been quite straight till now. But she was just warming him up. She closed the file, got up from her seat and walked behind him. He froze, not knowing what she had in mind. The fitted pants and shirt on a policewoman were quite intimidating for the man who sat in a loser's position in the small cubicle, with one blood-red coloured bulb that only threw light on the table. With him sitting in the chair and her standing behind him in the dark, he was visibly petrified.

'I—I did not kill her,' he stammered a little. Saima could see that he had gathered a pool of gall to utter those words.

He was pleading in a way that she wanted to believe him. It was just his alibi that threw him back in the barracks.

'Where were you yesterday morning?' She gave him the feeling that she was quite untouched by his statement.

He exhaled heavily before beginning the statement he had already given five times to five different officers. One of them had even recorded it on a video camera.

'It was Friday, yesterday, so it was my last day in the office for the week. I had some data sheets to fill for the week's record, that I had been putting off. The boss would have created a ruckus if I hadn't sent him the work that day so I woke up at around 5 a.m. Azra was sleeping so I left her in the bedroom and quietly went outside in the sitting room to work on the laptop.'

He took a pause and cleared his throat. Saima noticed his lips were as dry as an old shoe shrivelling up in the sun.

'Here.'

She passed him a small bottle of water that he readily accepted. His eyes flickered over her face for the briefest of moments. She had a feeling he was reading her face as much as she was reading his. She was ready to give him the smallest proportion of the benefit of doubt because he might…just might…be innocent. But even then, she was certain that he was a very shrewd man. She had heard him speak of the previous day, before, but she was giving him another chance to tell it. Maybe he would try to mend some of the conscious or unconscious errors in the story.

'Just around 8.30 a.m., I woke Azra up so she could make my morning tea, for I had to leave for office. She did that while I took a shower, dressed up and packed my office belongings. We had tea together.'

'Together? You mean you both were at close distance?' Saima interrupted him.

'Yes,' he answered thoughtfully.

'Did you notice any change in her? Behaviourally, or in her appearance?' She was relentlessly asking questions.

Saleem took a long pause and finally said, 'She looked fine. Then I left for the office.'

'Exactly what time was it when you left?' Saima was walking around the table, her eyes fixed on Saleem.

'I usually leave at 8.45 a.m.'

'I did not ask about the usual. I asked about *that day*.' She hovered over the table and her tone demanded from him to understand and answer her questions appropriately.

'It was between 8.45 and 8.50!' he said; the words erupting from his mouth.

'When you left her, what was the last conversation between you?'

He pondered for a moment. 'I told her I was getting late because of her and she told me to drive carefully,' he answered. 'I reached office just in time. It was going to be a busy day so I could not call her all day.'

He continued, 'I reached home at 5.15 p.m. as always and

found her on the living room floor.'

He stopped.

'How did you assess that she was dead?' the inspector asked.

'I felt for her pulse on the wrists. I touched her neck and checked for a heartbeat, but there was none. I shook her by the arms and also sprinkled water on her.'

'Okay, Saleem, answer this—you agree if I assume the distance between your office and home can be covered in fifteen minutes, even if it is the rush hour at five?'

'That's the time it takes me every day.'

Inspector Saima yet had her last question to ask. 'You know, my team has interviewed every single one of your colleagues, including your boss. So be honest, I need to ask you, where were you between 3.00 and 3.40 p.m., yesterday?'

'I was in the office.'

'But your colleagues, especially Waseem who sits in the cubicle next to yours, says you weren't in the seat for these forty minutes, approximately...maybe even earlier, because he says he noticed that you were missing when he wanted to talk to you about the feasibility report at 3.00 p.m. He also says he had to wait for you and it was not until 3.45 or so, when he saw you in your seat.'

'I—'

'Also, we asked the peon who brings you tea and he told us you had walked in through the entrance of the office somewhere between 3.40 to 3.45 p.m. and had asked him for a cup of tea. He remembers the time because he was leaving the building for his Asr namaz and had to stay back for your cuppa.'

## Saima

'Yes,' he said briefly.

'So, Saleem…' Saima had stopped encircling the prey and had stood right in front of him, ready to dig her claws so deep that it would hurt. 'Do you think forty-five minutes is enough time to commit a murder?'

'I DID NOT DO IT!' he said, his voice rising.

Saima banged her fist on the table and raised her voice five times louder than his, 'THEN WHO DID?'

'I don't know!'

'Where in the world were you during those forty-five minutes?'

He stayed silent.

'Saleem, this is your chance to plead guilty so that this can be over for both of us.' She was done questioning him.

'I was on the roof of the building,' he said quietly.

'What?' The inspector was not expecting this.

'I was on the roof of the building. The office is on the fourth floor of NPS Tower. The roof is above the sixth. I was there.'

'Is there anyone who can confirm this for you?'

'No,' he sounded fallen, like a man who had lost something.

'Why have you been omitting this from the story?'

He just shook his head.

'I took the stairs, not the elevator. I stayed there for around forty-five minutes, smoked and came back.'

'Why didn't you smoke in the balcony of the office?'

'I…I wanted to be alone for a while.'

'And why is that?'

'I don't know, okay? I don't know! But I was only up on

the roof, smoking bloody cigarettes!'

'So, you are telling me that if I go up on the rooftop of the NPS building, I shall find cigarette stubs from yesterday with your fingerprints on them?'

'No, I...I threw them over the railing, on the ground.'

'And why did you do that?' Saima had chosen to sit on the chair facing Saleem and had folded her arms over her chest.

'It's something I just do. I don't have an answer to that,' he snapped.

The inspector received a beep on her cell phone. She saw that it was her deputy inspector, Rehana, who was watching the investigation from the CCTV camera in the room next door.

'So, you were alone on the rooftop for all of those forty-five minutes?'

'Yes,' he nodded, his head bent over his chest.

'Did someone see you go up there?'

'I took the stairwell.'

'And how does that answer my question?' She bore her eyes into his face, angry at the indirect way he chose to reply.

'The stairwell is the most deserted place in the office. Everyone is in such a hurry all the time...no one uses it.'

'And that is why you chose to take it so that no one could see you?'

'Yes,' he nodded. 'I wanted to be alone,' he added hastily.

Inspector Saima saw her cell phone give a flicker of light again, when it beeped for the second time. She rose, and saw his eyes follow her.

'No, Saleem, we are not quite done with you,' she said, reading

## Saima

the query in his eyes and responding before he could utter it. She knocked at the huge metal door, which someone opened from the outside after making sure that it was the inspector knocking. She left the suspect in the cold and grave-like room. Her deputy had been pressing her through text messages to come and have a look at the forensic report. She walked out of the room with a resounding hitch in her brain, believing, for no apparent reason, that there was something missing from his story. She needed someone to make him spit out the missing forty minutes of the alibi. Also, she was sure about one thing—his version of the account was extremely glitch-free and well-rehearsed. She wondered, at times, whether he was speaking from a script. Each time he had used the same sequence and the same words to tell his story. In her code book, it was not right. He had been jumpy before the questioning began and suddenly, the quiver from his voice vanished when he had to relate the account.

Rehana, a big and stout lady in her early forties, was more than a decade older to her young boss, but she had been hired by the police force through a channel different than Saima's. Saima had taken the competitive exams for a position in the women's police department, while Rehana had been hired after being chosen from a long list of candidates who had applied for the job. Even though she wasn't physically as fit as a police person should be, Saima had found her to be efficient, hardworking and a woman who was not only earning bread for her family but also someone who was out there to prove herself.

She was more 'manly' than any other woman in the police station. Her bulk was more muscle than fat and that made her a

*Unfettered Wings*

towering deputy who was more scary to the juniors than the boss.

She was handed over the forensic report and it only added more questions to the case instead of answering any.

'There is nothing new in the investigation?' Rehana asked a rhetorical question. Saima looked at her briefly and shook her head.

'Leave it, Sir. Leave him to me. I am going to smack him a couple of times and he will blurt out the truth like a talking parrot.' Rehana sincerely felt the disappointment conveyed through Saima's expressions and wanted to mend it.

'Rehana, it's not as simple as that. We will get the forty-five minute story from him; that's not a problem.' Saima took a deep breath. 'The nature of the crime saddens me, hugely,' she added.

Rehana took the report out of the envelope and offered it to her boss. 'Maybe, this will help?'

**PRIME LABS**
PRIME LABS LIMITED,
KASHMIR HIGHWAY, SECTOR C5/8,
ISLAMABAD-4590
www.primelabs.com.pk

**FORENSIC REPORT**
Officer in case: Inspector Saima Akram
Client: Federal Police Force, Women's Station, Islamabad

> Police Reference: PL675009
> Laboratory Reference: AX7 V789
> Lab Scientist: Mohammad Aslam
>
> **Report: Death of Azra Bhatti, w/o Saleem Bhatti, unknown circumstances, on 15 July 2016 (Friday)**
> Blood serum was obtained from the dead body of Azra w/o Saleem, post death.
> Body was searched for fingerprints.
> Saliva was obtained to test for poisonous intake.
>
> **Results:**
> Body of the subject bore fingerprints that matched her own and of her husband Saleem Bhatti. Particularly on the arms and waist.
> Mild residue of acetaminophen (common painkiller drug) found on the tongue of the subject.
> Two teacups were found, with one bearing DNA traces of Saleem's saliva. Other cup has subject's fingerprints but no residue.
> Blood samples from the subject's body did not signify any insertion of poisonous chemical into the blood stream. The lungs of the deceased indicate some kind of carbon dioxide poisoning.
>
> **CAUSE OF DEATH:** UNKNOWN

'Have you followed up on the scene?' Saima was intrigued by the details in the report.

'Team A has already reached the scene,' Rehana replied dutifully.

Saima nodded. It was 6 p.m. and it had been twenty-four hours since the woman had been dead. Yet, her team, and she, had not been able to grasp at even one clue that could lead to the answer.

'See if you can make him speak.' She gestured towards the metal door behind which Saleem awaited his fate.

'You mean, there's more to him?' Rehana had made sure he was covered completely, before moving forward with the forensics.

'His story doesn't seem complete, you know? It just doesn't sound okay that he did not have time to call his wife but he kept smoking in solitude on the rooftop with no one to see him for forty minutes...' Saima's voice trailed off as she thought of something. 'The building he works in, has an underground parking, doesn't it?'

Rehana knitted her brows a little and responded thoughtfully, 'Yes, I think so.'

'Good, go send Team B to the parking. Ask them to shed their uniforms and go in civvies. Let them check if the valet or the ticket-puncher saw Saleem entering or exiting the building. Look for CCTVs in the elevators. Follow his trail through all of yesterday. And you my lady,' she spoke kindly to her subordinate, 'you look into him. Maybe he will talk more,' she instructed.

Rehana saluted her boss to bid farewell for the day, for she knew the young inspector had two kids—six and three years of age—who she needed to pay attention to. She stood erect until

## Saima

Saima left and then, it was time to relax just a little.

She picked up the phone, called in her junior staff, assembled Team B and assigned them the parking lot. She called in the peon, asked him to bring in a cup of tea along with a lamb-mince kachori. Just before her snacks arrived, she sat herself in the huge leather chair, unbuckled her belt to loosen her flabby belly and sighed in relief.

Inspector Saima had additional responsibilities to being a policewoman. Her husband, too, was a police officer in the main police lines, and her children—a son and a daughter—had to be given attention and be loved and cared for.

She reached her house in the private car given to her, along with a chauffeur—all three were government-maintained. The gatekeeper let the car in and the housemaid peeped through the blinds on the kitchen window. She shouted to the kids watching TV, that their mother was home. As soon as she stepped down from the car, her kids came rushing like a spurt of water and wrapped themselves around her legs. She picked up the younger one and he crawled down her back like a huge caterpillar. She had to hold his foot above her shoulder so he could have a safe landing. All the mental and physical fatigue her body had been through, evaporated into thin air with the cackles of her son and the shrieks of her daughter, who was telling her how well she did in the taekwondo class at school.

It was difficult to lend an ear to both of them at once, but women, when they become mothers, seem to get superpowers that allow them to multitask. She carried her son in her arms while listening to all the times his sister had teased him and hit him playfully on his tiny butt. Her daughter, too, was ranting about how 'stupid' she looked in the piggy tails the maid had made for her. Among this chaos, she entered the house, greeted the maid, asked about her husband and enquired what was for dinner.

'Daal chawal,' the maid answered.

'Asif won't be happy about that,' thought Saima. She didn't say anything to the maid, but only asked her to take out the lamb brains from the freezer.

'I will cook,' she told her with a smile. 'Just prepare the masala for me.'

Saima's beloved husband, Asif, was quite a foodie. Although the humble daal chawal would have made a sufficient dinner, yet, she wanted him to be pleased at the table after a long day's work.

'Could you get me a cup of tea?' she politely asked the maid, knowing well that at home she was not a police lady but a domestic woman who was grateful to another, for running her house, feeding her children and making her life more comfortable than most others. She spent an hour with the children, looking at her tiny preschooler's colouring efforts and applauding him for it. Along with this, she also stirred the sautéed onions, tomatoes, garlic and ginger, before adding the defrosted lamb brains to the saucepan. Saima had everything under control in her house within half an hour of entering it.

She suddenly heard her kids squeal harder than they had for their mother. Saima and the maid shared a smile.

'Bhaijan is here!' The maid gave words to their silent communication.

## Saima

'Yes.' She said, hurriedly checking her reflection in the stainless steel lid of the saucepan and then sailing out of the kitchen.

Asif, her husband, was more than a husband to her. He was the man she befriended at the police academy and had fallen in love with. He was handsome, moustached, courageous and a thorough professional. He was the man-in-uniform, who made women a little weak in the knees. He had had the same effect on his wife, who now reached out to kiss her husband amid protests from the kids that 'Papa was theirs alone'.

Dinner with the family was pleasant as always. They asked each other how everything was at the office but they had vowed not to drag the crime stories to the home, especially in front of the kids. He stretched on the sofa, watching the day's game, and she did her job of putting the kids to sleep. Later, she sat on the sofa, beside her husband, who threw an arm around her shoulders.

'You got any closer?' He was careful to not tread on her pride.

'I am not sure,' she said, looking up in the air.

Asif brought her closer and made her forget the stiffness of the day, for they both had only a limited time of privacy.

Later in the night, with the day done, Saima took silent refuge in the bathtub—the place where she did most of her thinking.

A hot tub, with rose oil and a little saffron, was good enough to soothe her tired muscles and aching head. She began thinking about Saleem. The stout, dark, fidgety man, who had had all of her attention for the past two days, was hiding something.

She had asked her team to report to her via SMS, whenever they got a breakthrough in the case. Team A had reported back, saying that the kitchen in Azra's home contained a cooking stove that worked on a gas cylinder attached to it. The valve that let the gas in, had been taken under custody and sent to the lab for forensic testing to determine the prints on it. Team B had sent a text, confirming that the valet did not see Saleem leave the building until after closing time. They had also checked the rooftop and found cigarette stubs, but the fingerprints on them would not be known until tomorrow morning, with a new forensic report. Her rookie had texted her, too, saying that the cell phones of both husband and wife had not revealed any communication that day. Saima had texted back, asking her to get the phone records from their respective mobile companies so they could see beyond deleted call logs. Rehana had texted her, too, reporting that Saleem had told her the story again, without any alteration. She said that she had also smacked him a few times, in the hope of him blurting out the truth, but it did not yield any results.

Thinking hard about her next step, she closed her eyes. Sometimes she thought she had bitten off more than she could chew. Sometimes, she felt that what her family members had warned her about police work being too hard, was true. However, what kept her going, was the fear of letting herself down in front of all those people who advised her against the job. She had taken a competitive exam to get into this profession. Now, she wanted to do justice to it. She was heading the women's wing of the federal police in the capital city of Islamabad. Being the

## Saima

first woman to be given charge of a whole fleet of policewomen who looked up to her, put more responsibility on her shoulders and probably that is why she felt the pressure more than it was in reality; she felt judgemental eyes on her when the culprit was not being revealed.

The next day, the rookie was waiting for Inspector Saima with the phone records from the mobile service providers. She had highlighted a few numbers on one of the spreadsheets.

'These,' the rookie said, pointing them out to her boss, 'are the phone records from Azra's cell phone. She did not have a record for this number in her cell phone.'

'Which means she kept deleting it,' Saima observed, her eyes fixated on the printed paper. The phone records were taken for the previous month, when Azra had not yet been married. The number that the rookie had highlighted, appeared four to five times every day in Azra's records and she had received it at least twice on the day she had died.

'Did you check whose number this is?' Saima's interest was piqued.

'Yes, sir. It is a boy named Shahbaz. I checked him out and he is Saima's neighbour. I have asked Team A to bring him in today.'

'Well, are they en route?'

'They will be here in no time,' the rookie answered.

'Good work!' She smiled at her junior, who blushed with pleasure but kept her face poker straight and her expression, sober.

'Thank you, Sir.' She straightened up to greet her superior, who was leaving the staff room to go to her own office. 'Just tell me when Shahbaz is here,' said Saima, giving her a last order before going inside her official dome.

❦

'I loved her, you understand? I loved her more than anyone could ever love a person.' Shahbaz was visibly agitated and angry when Rehana started questioning him. Saima watched from the CCTV.

'Why did you call her yesterday?' the enormous assistant inspector asked him. She did not have the patience of Inspector Saima and chances were, if he created a lot of trouble, he was going to have the worst thrashing of his life.

'I have been calling her every day, for the past three years. I could not BREATHE without talking to her, you get that? You have a record for what? One month? Two? I have been there in her life for three years. That bastard of a man—that cheap Saleem—could not keep her alive even for a week?'

His mouth was foaming and his eyes were spitting fire. He lunged forward over the table.

Rehana was still unmoved. 'What did you talk about?'

'I received a missed call from her in the middle of the night, two nights ago. I didn't want to respond, knowing she must be with her husband. Next morning around six, I called her. I know she wakes up early for the morning namaz, so I thought she might be alone and could take my call.'

'You mean the day she died?'

His eyes gained a red hue and his mouth drooped. He fought

## Saima

back his tears so as not to appear weak, and nodded.

'Yes,' he said briefly.

'Well?' Rehana prompted.

'She said a week into her marriage, she could not stand the man she slept with. She said she wanted to put an end to her life.'

'You mean suicide?'

'Yes, and I tried all I could to talk her out of it. She was crying on the phone. It was hard talking to her like that, but I did my best.'

'You think she committed suicide?'

'That is for you to find out, officer,' he almost snarled.

'But,' he added, 'you need to check on Saleem. That creep is what made things end up the way they are today. Suicide or not, she was stifled by him. She called him "filth". Ask him, ask HIM!'

'I know my job, and now you shut the hell up, Romeo.' Rehana had enough of the emotional dramatics and she rose to leave. She signalled into the camera that she was done.

Once outside, Rehana had put a report on Inspector Saima's table within thirty minutes. The findings of teams A and B, as well as her investigations in the cell with Saleem and Shahbaz, were all in the report. Team A had filed the forensic report about the gas valve, which only had Azra's fingerprints on it. The information was not very helpful since those prints could have been made when she was preparing tea, or even before that. The carbon monoxide detector had not traced any gaseous residue. Rehana had also cracked open the secret of Saleem's forty-five minutes—he had been engaged in a secret meeting on the roof with a representative of the rival software company and was selling the blueprint of his company's designs for a steep price. He claimed he needed the money to take Azra on a honeymoon, since he was broke after the wedding expenses. The buyer was sought out, questioned, and Saleem's story was found to be true. His alibi cleared him, much to Saima's disappointment. Rehana had also filed the reports of her questioning sessions with Azra and Shahbaz's families, revealing the fact that that they both were lovers during their college days, and Azra had been forced into getting married to Saleem by her family.

Saima decided to put Shahbaz through one more round of questioning. She had demanded her team to withhold his cell phone (which he was reluctant to part with), his laptop and any other device he might be using. She got the memory cards read and found several pictures of Azra before her wedding. The gadgets came out clean, except for some harmless photographs. He, too, was freed, but she did put some feelers on him.

Saima was getting a sinking feeling. She could not let a human's death go in vain just because she had not been efficient enough to find the loophole the killer would had left behind. She remembered her trainers in the police academy saying, 'There is always a clue. Always.' She scanned the files and reports in front of her. She had already been through all of them many times, but still felt there was something she had missed. She read and read until the sight of the reports became repulsive to her. There was still an hour to go till the time she usually left office. She wanted to go see the dead girl at the morgue. That was one thing she had personally missed having done till now.

Once again, she gave charge of the station to Rehana, who

## Saima

accepted it readily. Rehana had had plans of getting a shoulder rub from one of the junior staff members since the beginning of the day, and was happy to salute a goodbye to her boss and occupy the chair she loved so much. She gathered all the papers Saima had left scattered on the table, made a file out of them and rested her legs on the table top. She ordered her tea and pakoras and got a shoulder rub and neck massage for the next half hour while she carefully read the details in the reports. She slammed the file back on the table a few hours later, and wiped the pakora grease from her hands on the back of the faux leather chair. She muttered a few curses at the murderer and the case itself, just before leaving the station around dinner time. She had cracked a few cases for Inspector Saima during her seven-year-old service, and always wanted to impress her boss. The helplessness regarding Azra's murder frustrated her beyond measure. She couldn't take it in like Saima and still put a sober face. She yelled at the juniors for being useless, walked out of the station and hoped Saima would find a clue at the morgue.

⁓

The mortuary was just like the rest of the hospital building—a stench followed Saima through the passage where the dead bodies were kept at freezing temperature. The eerie silence of the passage could have scared a faint-hearted woman, but the uniform Saima wore and the duty she upheld, were enough for her to be able to shun her fears. The attendant took her to the casket where Azra lay. She was dressed in a hospital gown, since the autopsy had to be be performed and samples had to be be taken. She had been handled by so many people before her last rituals could be carried out. While a dead woman should have been dressed in her kafan and buried in the ground by now, Inspector Saima blamed her own incompetence for the disgrace Azra's dead body had to undergo. She paid homage to her, recited the dua, asked for her forgiveness and signalled the attendant to take her back.

At home, she went through the same routine as the previous day. The maid was preparing chicken-and-cheese-stuffed parathas, so Saima didn't bother her for tea. She let the chatter of her kids ease out the aggravation of the day. When Asif came home, she forced a smile from the sofa but didn't jump to greet him. Dinner was filled with the discussion of the T20 cricket matches.

With the kids snuggled in bed, she came to sit down with her husband on the couch.

'What's wrong, Saima?' asked Asif, and put the TV on mute.

Saima took a long pause before answering, 'The case...'

'Can I help?' He had wanted to ask her this, because there were conjectures going around in the headquarters that the women's police station wouldn't be able to crack the homicide, and so the case should be transferred to the men's police station in the same locality. Asif was kind enough to never share the jokes the men at the head office made about the policewomen. He had known Saima ever since their training days at the police academy and had faith in her ability. However, her long face made him upset.

'I am sure it's in front of me,' she said, staring blankly at the TV screen.

'Of course, it is. And you will figure it out,' he said, going behind her. He put his broad hands on her shoulders and pushed her back towards the sofa, to recline.

'Tell me, what can I do?' he insisted.

Saima smiled. 'You honestly want to do something for me?'

'You need to ask that?'

'Well, actually there is something I want you to do.'

'I am listening…' Asif gave her his full attention and sat beside her.

'Well, after all the humdrum of the day, I still haven't gotten my cup of tea.' She wore a serious expression but the humour danced like a flame in her eyes.

He stared at her briefly and then threw back his head to laugh.

'Alright, Sir,' he teased her playfully.

Minutes later when they both sat on the couch, Saima was silently appreciating the weak-coloured, but fragrant tea her husband had doused with cardamom, cinnamon and cloves.

She suddenly froze halfway through finishing her drink. She stared at the prints her lipstick had made around the rim of the cup and almost dropped the ceramicware from her hands.

Asif was engrossed in the reruns of the match and was quite oblivious of his wife's eureka moment. She almost beat herself up for not noticing such a glitch. She jumped up, dressed up in whatever her hands could grab from the wardrobe and seized the keys to her car.

'Where—what's wrong?' Asif was startled by the sudden chaos.

'It's alright. I will be back in half an hour.' She was in a tearing hurry.

'But listen—wait—Saima!'

Asif couldn't stop her as she raced away. By the time he came to the threshold of the house, she had sped away in the car. Asif turned back to look at the kids' bedroom door and decided to wait before jumping into his own car.

On her way, she called a sleeping Rehana to meet her at Saleem's house. She could hear her whine but she barked that it was an order.

She knew from the beginning that something was wrong with the husband. She checked to see if she was carrying the sanctioned pistol with her in the dashboard and was pleased to see she was armed in case of any misadventure. Outside his house, she waited for Rehana to reach. She came in an autorickshaw, her hair, wild, and her face as swollen as a water balloon.

They rang the bell and waited for him to answer.

'Who is it?'

'Open up, Saleem!'

'Who is it?' he repeated.

'It's your mother, bloody rascal! Open up or I will burn this place down!' Poor Rehana was taking out the anger from her sleep deprivation, on Saleem.

He opened the door a little but tried to lock it when he saw who the ladies were. Rehana's bulky frame came in handy when she put her full strength on the door and forced it open. Saleem toppled backward.

## Saima

'What, you lost confidence in your script?' Saima spoke through gritted teeth.

She ordered Rehana to pick him up and make him sit on a chair. Rehana brought his hands together behind him and put a handcuff on his wrists. She then pointed her pistol to his head so he wouldn't move.

'Now tell me, Saleem, how did you do it?'

'I did not do it!'

She came closer to face him and told him this was his last chance to confess.

'If you are not ready, let me make it easier for you, you useless bit of junk. You never woke up early that day. You were sleeping when Azra awoke for her morning prayer. She went into the bathroom to speak to her lover Shahbaz, where she was crying.' Saima jutted her neck to catch a glimpse of the bedroom and its adjoining bathroom. 'Seeing that the bathroom is quite near to the bed, you must have heard her talk.'

'However...' she stopped in mid-sentence and walked into the bedroom. She entered the bathroom, examined it and came out after a few seconds. 'However, Saleem, you did not interrupt her conversation. You heard her tell Shahbaz that she would commit suicide, AND you heard her call you "filth".'

Saleem was listening to every word and the colours of his face were changing as rapidly as his heartbeat was speeding up.

'So,' Saima continued, 'when she came out, you either dragged her into the living room, or waited until she came out herself. What paraphernalia you used, is something you shall tell me, but I have no doubt that you suffocated her. Didn't you?'

'With a pillow?' Rehana chirped in.

'No, Rehana. This is not a horror movie. This is worse. He did it with something that left no mark, residue or swelling on her face. What was it, Saleem?'

Saleem dropped his head, but lifted it up when Rehana kicked him in the shin and he whimpered, 'Cling film.'

'Cling film! Right! That makes sense,' Saima said thoughtfully. 'You wrapped it over her nose and mouth from behind her? That way, a sudden blockade of air cavities causes death through carbon dioxide poisoning.' She threw him a hateful look and kicked him in the groin. He yelped like a dog.

'And the tea was a good touch,' Saima was thinking out aloud. 'You know, Rehana, when we read the first forensic report, it told us there and then, that this filthy roach was the killer.'

'Really?' Rehana was wide awake by now. The twist in the story had heightened her adrenaline.

'It said that there was saliva residue on one cup and that belonged to Saleem but the other, with Azra's fingerprints, had no residue. This smartass knew well enough to put Azra's prints on the cup while she lay dead but he forgot to brush the rim across her lips.'

Rehana slapped him a few times until Saima asked her to stop. 'She was never alive to share that cup of tea with you. While you, heartless piece of crap, you had the guts to kill someone's daughter, drink a cup of tea over her dead body, dress up and leave for office, and sell your company's secrets for a tip.' The hatred in Saima's voice and on her face was reflective of the despise she felt for the criminal.

## Saima

'What were you going to do with the money, huh? What? Run away?' Her question was rhetorical.

'Rehana!' She commanded her to call up the headquarters and ask for backup as well as a vehicle to carry him to the main police lines where the policemen could get the whole story out of him in his words. They were both waiting when she saw a familiar car screech and halt in front of Saleem's house.

It was Asif.

'How...?' Saima was pleased, surprised and grateful at the same time.

'Car tracker, babe.' He leaned in closer to pat her shoulder.

'Good work, officer,' he said, looking at Rehana and commending her, too. They waited for around twenty minutes with the murderer tied on the chair until the policemen arrived. They watched him being taken away. Inspector Saima sighed with relief but also with pain, for the young girl had just got married and was killed for honour. She stood there for a while in silence when Rehana bleated from behind, 'Can I go home now, sir?'

Saima broke into peals of laughter. Rehana and Asif both looked confused but Saima knew how hard it was for Rehana to wake up in the middle of the night and do police work. 'Yes, go Rehana and take the day off tomorrow.'

'Really?' She was as happy as a kid getting an extra holiday.

'Yes, really. And can I ask for something?'

'Your wish is my command, Sir.' She was taken aback a little.

'Let's get over with this "Sir" business. Call me "Inspector".'

'Yes, Inspector.'

'Nah,' said Saima, putting her arm around her plump and

short subordinate. 'Off-duty, we are friends.'

'Wow!' Rehana was happier than a young boy on a beach.

Asif asked his wife which car she wanted to drive and she answered, 'Let's go home together. Rehana can take my car.'

'Forever?' Rehana asked jokingly, and Saima laughed. She sat beside her partner in peace after a long bout of consternation.

# Beena
### *Love me like Shah Rukh Khan*

Beena was staring at the thin line of twilight peeping into her room through the glass window. The beige-coloured curtains were as old as her marriage and had become a little crooked around the corners with age. The glow of the dawn was gradually getting brighter and the darkness inside her bedroom was getting eaten up by the mellow yellowness of the morning sunshine.

Her alarm would not beep until after a few more minutes. She was surprised at how mechanical her sleep pattern had become—she could even get a two-hour sleep at night and still beat her alarm clock in the morning. Beena brought out her tiny beeper from under the pillow for the umpteenth time saw that she still had five extra minutes before she had to get out of the bed. She wrapped the blanket fiercely around herself one last time, ducked her head inside the warm, fleece bedcover and tightly shut her eyes.

She could listen to the breathing sounds her husband was making. He lay just a few inches away from her on the other side of the bed. She smiled a little to herself when she realized how accustomed she had grown to his breathing pattern during the five years of their marriage. He turned on his side, facing her and she looked at his face like a teenage girl would look at her crush. His large nose, big eyes covered by long, thick eyelashes, and a set of full lips, were proportioned very handsomely under a broad forehead.

His hair was greying a little near the temples. He always voiced a little too much concern over the silver growing on his head at thirty-five, but she secretly loved the age on him. As her eyes searched his face, she resisted the urge to stroke his stubble. He was very hairy, almost like a big teddy bear, and his stubble, awfully rough, grew almost overnight. She imagined his coarse chin scratching her cheek. The feeling made her tremble with ecstasy, and that is when the beeper went off.

The sound was set to low, so the beep was quite muffled under the pillow. She got up gently from the mattress, since the bed (which she had received in her dowry) had started to creak a little. It was still early for her husband, Irfan, to wake up. She wanted him to get that bonus half hour of sleep which he deserved.

Tiptoeing to her son's bedroom, she made a brief stopover in the kitchen. She had to use the electric kettle to heat up the water since the frequent load-shedding had made it impossible for the geyser to work in the middle of winters. And splashing cold water on her preschooler's face was out of question. With the moody toddler awoken and dressed for school, he was force-fed half a boiled egg that had been cooked over an electric stove. Just before she grabbed her son's satchel to fill it with store-bought cupcakes, packets of crisps and a small carton of juice, she turned on the knobs on the cooking range. It was an attempt to check if it was working. She was already feeling ashamed for being a bad mother by giving her son a lunch comprising packaged food.

The cooking range was barren and unresponsive to the glow of the lighter, so maybe she could feel a little less guilty. She smiled at her little boy, Sameer, who was yawning while dressed in his cadet uniform. Just before she left, she mentally checked off her to-do list and grabbed the car keys from the mantelpiece. She was careful in opening the click-lock of the main door lest it should awaken Irfan, and put it back even more gently. In the car, Sameer had already started to whine, for his mother (who had hardly put the key in the ignition) had not yet started playing the songs of his choice. This meant that while keeping her eyes on the rear-view mirror, one hand on the steering wheel, a foot on the clutch and the other on the brakes, she had to use her free hand to fiddle with the buttons of the car stereo, switch it from Irfan's news channel on AM, to the CD for Sameer, and let the speakers blare the annoyingly catchy *Paw Patrol* song. Throughout the drive, she was so engrossed in planning out her day that she barely noticed herself humming along the tune of the cartoon even when Sameer had hopped away to school and she had reached home.

She was a doctor by profession—a gynaecologist, to be

precise. The public hospital at which she worked, housed two-hundred beds in the maternity ward. Although she was only one of the forty-three doctors at the Obstetrics and Gynaecology department, she knew she was indispensible. The patients outnumbered the doctors, every day. In such a situation, it was very tough to take a day off. However, she had a plan under her belt for an upcoming special occasion.

She had been in doubt ever since she woke up as to whether Irfan would remember their wedding anniversary coming up on the weekend. He had always been forgetful of dates, but she had plans to surprise him in his office. Every anniversary, she had waited for him to bring home a present or even a single rose bud. Her dreams were quite simple and small. She did not expect candlelight dinners and expensive gifts. She rather expected a loving embrace. To her, going to the cinema was more romantic than shopping at a posh mall. She made it a point to make Irfan understand her simple approach towards life, right after they were married. How successful she had been with that, is another story, for another time.

The wedding, too, was a homely affair. They had gotten their nikah done at Beena's father's house. She was that sort of a girl; one who wanted to get married in her father's house in simple attire, with a handful of guests to celebrate her happiness. Irfan's family had scrunched up their noses at the idea of the wedding plan, for they had wanted some pomp and show for the youngest son. Luckily for Beena, Irfan loved her enough to sacrifice the glitz his family had planned for him.

Beena had known Irfan ever since she had started working

## Beena

at the Children's Charity Clinic adjacent to the law firm where Irfan worked. He was one of the corporate lawyers and she got assigned to him as the intern who would fetch files, take printouts and make photocopies for the lawyer who represented the clinic. It was while working on a case that Irfan and she became friends and very soon, more than that. By the end of her MBBS, she was a bride who was taken into a household with a new set of people and had a lot to understand and a lot more to let go of. Even things that meant very much were let slip within days so that her mind and her heart could be emptied for new relationships, new aspirations and new dreams.

It was Irfan's good luck that Beena's dreams were simple. She was moulded from emotions rather than ambitions. She yearned for appreciation, a word of love, a night-in with her husband on the weekend, snuggled underneath a warm sheet and watching TV. It didn't matter what was playing on the TV as long as she was with him, but if someday she would catch a telecast of a song or movie starring Shah Rukh Khan, it would be blissful.

Her one-sided 'relationship' with the actor had a history—she had watched a blurry broadcast of the drama, *Fauji*, on Doordarshan at her father's house in her teenage and had instantly fallen in love with the dusky Pathan looks of Khan. It had started off like an average crush—posters appearing in the bedroom, newspaper cuttings of the hero in the daily journal she wrote, a collection of cassettes with songs featuring him, and repetitively sneaking out from college with friends to watch multiple reruns of *Dilwale Dulhaniya Le Jayenge*.

The first movie she watched with Irfan in the privacy of

their bedroom was the same. Irfan had yawned throughout, for he had watched the movie once before, but Beena would still laugh at the scenes that had made her laugh before, still cry and get fidgety when the heroine could not grab Shah Rukh's hand to get on to the train... Irfan was less amused by the movie and more by his wife's antics. Every now and then, he would punctuate his silence with a remark about Shah Rukh's 'over-acting' or his 'childish character' which made her a little annoyed. But she believed that it was her man getting jealous. So she would laugh out to assure him she was still on his side.

'Men!' she would think, chuckling silently. She never quite told Irfan that his nose was somewhat similar to that of Shah Rukh's. As soon as she had laid eyes on her husband, she had made that connection between the lawyer and her crush.

Now when five years had passed since he had become her husband, she wanted to add a little dash of romance to her otherwise mechanical life by rekindling the strong bond of love they shared, at their fifth wedding anniversary. She was thoughtlessly going through the routine of the day, sending her husband off to work and busying herself with all that demanded attention from her at home. In between chores, she made it a point to book a private booth at the posh cinema her neighbour had been bragging about having been to, since last month. A new movie with Shah Rukh in the lead was about to have its worldwide release on the weekend and her anniversary fell a day later. What better way to have fun than go explore the coolest cinema in Lahore, munch on toffee-coated popcorn, hold hands with the man she loved and gaze at the man who had quickened her heartbeat for the first time. She wanted the evening show so they could later go to a restaurant for dinner.

Beena was a wise spender, but for the past two months she had been especially stingy with the house kitty. Saving up was not easy, with growing responsibilities concerning Sameer. He was out of diapers and feeders, but at his age, she realized she needed more of everything to keep him happy—food, toys, clothes and time. However, her small efforts, such as buying a two-litre canister of cooking oil instead of three, or adding water to her shampoo bottle to make it last just a little longer, had made things a bit easier for her.

That afternoon, when Beena went to pick her son from school during her lunch break, she switched on the radio channel in her car that played the latest Indian and Pakistani songs, enjoyed every moment of it and grinned ear to ear, for she had booked a cubicle at the cinema, engaged her mother to look after Sameer when she would go out on the date with Irfan and bought enough grocery to make a feast of a lunch for everyone at Irfan's office. She had worked there and knew they all loved biryani and korma. Her freezer was stocked and the prints from the online ticketing service for Shah Rukh's new movie were in her wallet. Besides, a table for two at the local cafe was awaiting their arrival on Saturday. She had only managed to book a table at the cafe that served soup and pasta (nothing fancy but it was enough for them). She had everything under control.

Irfan had sensed the extra wide grin on his wife's face later in the evening and had believed that it was simply because she was a happy person. He silently congratulated himself for being such an excellent husband for making his wife glow for no apparent reason. Beena, however, was assured that he had no inkling about the anniversary date again. She kept silent, too. Even if he couldn't remember dates, she wasn't going to spoil a celebration-worthy occasion for herself. She knew she would put in a lot of effort for cooking a luncheon for Irfan and his staff, and the restaurant booking was her gesture of love towards Irfan. The movie, however, was a favour she had done to herself. Since Irfan would never make time or prefer to go watch a Shah Rukh movie on a weekend, she had planned it all out silently. It would be a good enough present from his side if he simply went along with her plan. That was all she wanted.

∼

On the day of the anniversary, she had called in sick at the hospital in the early hours of the morning, and confided in her best friend about her real plan. She felt the familiar pang of guilt once again, but reprieved herself from it, thinking that she deserved at least one day to herself.

Getting her friend to take care of her assignments at work, she had finished her chores earlier than usual after dropping off Sameer and saying goodbye to Irfan. She had toiled over the cylinder-run stove in the first half of the day, to cook the two favourite dishes of her husband and that, too, in massive proportions. At lunchtime, she had driven to the office to give him what she considered the best present of all—a flower. Irfan was surprised when she put a single bud of rose on his table at the office and handed over the huge picnic basket to the peon.

## Beena

A single rose is all she had wanted from him as an anniversary present. However, she bought one and gave it to him instead. It felt better than waiting for a rose from him; giving one was almost equally exhilarating. She left him with his colleagues, who had gathered around to congratulate them both. He offered to drop her till the exit or, at least, till the elevator, but she declined.

'Save it for tonight.' She smiled meaningfully at him and urged him to go play host for his colleagues. Feeling elated, for the plan was running smoothly, she double-checked her reservation at the cinema and felt ecstatic when she was told that cubicle 27 was reserved under her name and shall stay hers to claim until the first thirty minutes of the movie's beginning. After that, it would be sold off to the first customer on the waiting list.

Her next job was to pick Sameer from school, bring him home, and bathe and dress him. Before teatime, Beena dropped Sameer at his granny's house, got a facial, wax and a haircut. She looked great when she stepped out of the beauty parlour. She had ironed her and Irfan's clothes so they could leave for the cinema as soon as he was home.

Irfan came back to a perfumed, powdered and dressed-up wife who was embraced and fondled by the tired husband.

'How much time do we have?' He cocked his head to glance at the wall clock.

Beena saw the playful glimmer in his eyes and recognized the glimmer too well. She blushed a little, but told him they had no time to waste.

'What "waste", yaar?' he protested. 'I am talking about being your hero tonight.'

She laughed in response and shoved him into the shower, begging him to be dressed on time. After a few minutes, Beena asked him for the tenth time regarding what was taking him so long in there.

'The hot shower is not letting me go,' he sang in response.

'Irfan, please, hurry up,' she pleaded. Beena was getting restless by the second.

'Okay, okay, five more minutes. First you put me in competition with that Shah Rukh Khan and then don't even give me enough time to preen myself to beat him.'

'You know what?' He had walked out of the shower, water dripping from his torso, and the rest covered with a huge white towel. 'I can look better than him if I wear those Italian suits all the time,' he remarked, making her laugh uncontrollably.

Beena felt sorry for him. She came over, put her arms around his neck and kissed his chin. 'You look better than anyone, anytime,' she purred sweetly.

'Like, even now?' He made a bodybuilder's pose and smiled at her. She broke into cackles. Clearly, he was fooling around and needed no consolation. She knew he was slightly put-off by the intervention of Shah Rukh Khan in his little romantic programme, but he was playing along well. She chose not to say anything, but in her heart, she felt the gratitude. He took his time while Beena sat on the bed, biting her freshly-polished nails. Like one would help a baby, she aided him in getting dressed just to expedite the process.

Irfan couldn't help but notice the faint smile on his wife's face on the way to the cinema. He felt a little ashamed and guilty for not making her smile like that more often, but he refrained from saying anything. Beena was as excited as a college girl. The memory of standing in a long queue to buy tickets at a double price for Shah Rukh's movies during college days, had come back rushing to her mind. The mall in which the cinema was located was marvellous, but not enough to steal the limelight from the movie she was looking forward to watch with her husband, spending a few hours of privacy and contentment in his presence, the warmth of his hands rubbing across her own. The giddiness made her giggle as she stepped on the escalator that took her several floors above the ground to the classy cinema she had heard so much about.

The golden ceiling and red carpets in the theatre highlighted the ivory-coloured seats. It was indeed a privilege to be there. Beena and Irfan had settled down a good ten minutes early but they were quite upset when even after twenty minutes of the allotted time, the movie was not played. The theatre was full of confused people who doubted the efficacy of their wristwatches and were asking the time from strangers sitting next to them. Beena kept her positive vibe alive and supposed that the people operating the cinema must be prepping up the system. Maybe, they were waiting for a VIP. Maybe, they were still waiting for the hall to fill up. She had as many theories as the minutes that went ticking by. Half an hour later, a stout little man, suited and bespectacled, stood in front of the black drapes that covered the silver screen. He asked for a microphone from the floor manager and introduced himself as the cinema owner before saying, 'Ladies and gentlemen, I regretfully inform you that as per government orders, in light of the disturbance at the Line of Control between India and Pakistan, all Bollywood motion pictures have been banned from screening, until further notice. Please bring your punched tickets at the ticket booth for a full refund.'

―

Beena had been quiet throughout the dinner. She had no appetite, and the 'Pasta Napoleon' that Irfan had suggested to her, tasted bland. She kept tossing the noodle strips around in her plate. Irfan noticed her distress but stayed quiet. He knew it was not the movie but Beena's controlling nature that had been affected. He tried to make small talk with her about the food and the dessert he would order, but she wasn't very enthused about the conversation.

She couldn't help but notice; Irfan had a smug smile on his face. She brushed away the gloomy feeling that overtook her, for he had always felt jealous of Shah Rukh Khan. However, what she couldn't ignore was Irfan eyeing a beautiful young woman sitting right beside them. She was having coffee with a handsome young man, probably her boyfriend. Agitated, she picked up her phone just to check if she had a message. There was none, so she put it back and stared at the wallpaper—it was a selfie she had taken with Irfan asleep by her side. She stared at it for the longest time, with her chin resting on her palm and her other hand curled up in her lap. Without shifting her posture, she glanced up at Irfan who was still eyeing the girl with interest. Beena shut her eyes.

## Beena

She lectured herself inwardly to enjoy her husband's attention with or without the charm of Shah Rukh's movie to ignite the romance. Her brain argued back that she couldn't do any more than she already had. She had scolded her brain for being negative when he had come back home without a present or flower for her. Beena told herself he was only *looking* at the girl, and nothing worse.

The phone rang. It was her mother calling.

'Hello?' It was Sameer! He was still up! She assured him she was coming home sooner than expected and would pick him on the way. That attracted Irfan's attention and he pulled a face. He wanted some time alone with his wife. Beena ignored him.

'So, shall we go?' she asked her husband, who was wiping off the last bit of lasagne from his plate. His face showed disappointment.

'Yeah.' He stood up and slid his arm over her shoulders as they walked towards the car.

Usually they drove in silence, listening to a qawwali singer, who was Irfan's favourite. She found the music rather irritating. She was more of a ghazal fan. Beena turned off the music. Irfan kept it that way. He told her she was being dramatic.

That was his favourite word for every mood. Whenever Beena was upset about something at the hospital, when she cried buckets because she had helped deliver premature triplets, when she saw scratches on Sameer's arm made by the bully in the class—every single time, she was stamped with the same word—dramatic. She never reacted, but that night, Beena decided to make her point. She told him how irked she was with his ogling. And his cold personality. And the indifference. And being dramatic was better than being apathetic. Irfan had not quite expected such a turn of events. He blamed Shah Rukh for his wife's sudden mood swing.

'Don't you bring Shah Rukh into this!' she retorted.

'Why shouldn't I? You look for him in me, don't you?'

'I am not a teenager, Irfan. I know better than that,' she snapped. 'Don't point out my faults! Just accept that you are heartless.'

'Heartless? Why? Because I cannot sing songs in a garden for you?' Irfan had lost his cool, too.

'That is not the only way to express love,' Beena said calmly, hoping this would end the argument.

'I was like this when you met me, Beena. I have been like this. Maybe you need to redefine love for yourself.'

His rigidity broke her heart.

'Stop looking for filmi heroes and reel love in real life!' Irfan took advantage of her silence and continued his argument.

Beena leaned back and put her head on the headrest in utter annoyance.

'See, this is the problem. You want a filmi life. This is reality, Beena, no one is perfect…' Irfan continued.

He rambled on and on, telling Beena how imperceptive she was about the notions and realities of life, and how much she needed to learn.

Beena closed her eyes and let his words float out of the window without bothering her.

# Meera
### Professor Crank

The one thing that really messed with Meera's head was someone calling her 'Mrs Meera Malik'. She found it very presumptuous on their part to assume she was a missus.

'Miss,' she hissed every time that she had to correct them. Her sharp nose, arched eyebrows and thin lips accentuated her curt and crisp voice.

Meera Malik was a professor of Political Science. She had been teaching at the University of the Punjab for longer than most of her colleagues. So much so, unlike her peers, she remembered how the grandiose building of the varsity had been erected from scratch, on both sides of the Bambawali-Ravi-Bedian canal, popularly known as the BRB canal. Legend has it that the BRB had been built during the Mughal era. Ironically, the same canal that had run through the heart of Lahore during the days of the united subcontinent had served as a trench during the war of 1965 between the volatile neighbours. In its earliest days, the campus had been akin to the wild woods of Wonderland where Alice had lost herself. As of 2016, it was still enveloped with trees and bushes, but with a much-needed expansion—adding of educational divisions as modern as Gender Studies and Space Sciences, multiple hostels, roads and overhead bridges that connected the two segments of the varsity from across the BRB—the campus had become less dense in fauna and more populated with day and evening students, as well as boarders.

Despite all the advancements to its form, the university still reminded its old lovers of its earliest days. During that time, the Political Science department was one of the first to take on admissions. It was more popular and versatile. The teachers were public figures—a politician, a public speaker, a writer, a newspaper columnist. Those were the days when the faces and names of the teaching staff attracted the students, and not the subject that promised a well-salaried job. Those were the times when the ambition for education was philosophic and not monetary. It complimented the fact that our needs and requirements were lesser and simpler than the present.

Meera could compare those times to now because she was an aging icon of the department she served. She had retired five years ago, at the age of sixty-two, but the rest of the staff—comprising her students—had insisted that she keep an ad hoc position for the postgraduate and PhD students. Meera had willingly agreed. After all, she had given all her youth and age to the Political Science department as a teacher, instructor, adviser and chairperson...there had been different labels during

## *Meera*

the years. Other than her loyalty, the unavoidable fact was that she had nothing else to keep her as busy as the department did.

Staying single was a choice and she had defended that choice vehemently, whenever she could. Her father's house, in the Defence area of Karachi, was among one of the first bungalows to be built in the middle of nowhere, as soon as the war of 1947 was over. Those officers who had performed well, had been facilitated with medals, and been allotted pieces of land and other perks. This plot, given to Meera's father, Brigadier Shafat Malik, too, was one such privilege. Hailing from the rural town of Larkana in Sindh, Brigadier Malik had decided to move from the desert-like municipality and settle down into the metropolitan hub of Karachi. Defence areas in all major cities are undisputedly the poshest localities, with many architectural and infrastructural privileges. Karachi was no exception. The environs were structured in a way that one felt like some sort of royalty while residing in the area.

Meera had been brought up with the clichéd silver spoon in her mouth. She went to the best of schools, colleges, and even abroad, for higher studies. When she returned to Pakistan in the 1980s, she did not have to work hard to secure a job at Karachi University. A foreign qualification was not common in those days and Meera was luckier than she knew. Every time there was a suitor for marriage, she insisted on interviewing the boy herself and always ended up finding him below her expectations. For ten years, she had to face pressure from the family to get married, but as soon as she hit thirty-five, the proposals started dwindling and the pressure decreased. The rest of her siblings were married but their problems and grumbling only strengthened Meera's stance of not letting marriage ruin her life. She was told marriage was a love-hate relationship, but she was not ready to commit herself to such an unstable and insecure bondage.

Marred psychologically and teased by her family, she decided to move to Lahore, away from the people who kept asking her to pursue the road she wasn't quite impressed with. She had to wait for a year until her application was accepted by the University of the Punjab in Lahore so she could settle down in an annexe in the upscale locality of Defence, in Lahore.

As time went by, Meera filled her time with books, both reading and writing them. She wrote non-fiction, especially regarding political reforms. Her students admired her intelligence and idolized her. She had the likes of Machiavelli and Marx on the tips of her fingers. She could quote Orwellian literature to prove a political point and could get emotional while quoting from William Butler Yeats's nationalistic poetry. A verse from his poem, 'He Wishes for the Cloths of Heaven', carved in sandalwood, sat cosily atop her desk in her miniscule cabin at the department.

She had taught various sub-disciplines of the subject during all these years, but lately, she was taking the Bilateral Policy course for her PhD students. She had felt most gratified while teaching this lot—partly because they were at par with her intellectual yardstick and partly because everyone seemed to be confused about the concepts of bilateralism.

'Miss Malik, how can we protect our identity from cultural imperialism?'

## *Meera*

'What "cultural imperialism"? That's a myth you have entangled yourselves with.'

'You think the invasion of foreign culture into ours isn't an intended attack on our culture? That the idea behind the invasion is not imperialism?'

'Azhar, is it?'

Azhar, the student, nodded.

'Well, Azhar, the things that you take as the elements of "culture" are nothing but products that are being sold from one country to another. Everyone is not a buyer, you know? So stay put, no one is trying to enslave you or your culture.' Meera fixed her spectacles on her nose while the rest of the class chuckled.

Azhar was not one to give up.

'You can have your opinion, madam, but I still firmly believe that Indian movies, cartoons and soaps, their music and traditions, are causing undue harm to our culture and our youth.'

Meera opened her mouth to say something but Azhar was not yet finished. 'Also, the Western culture is disrupting our youth in a way that their correction has become impossible. It all started with McDonald's burgers, which looked harmless, and now look where the culture has taken us…porn, illicit relationships, unwedded mothers. That is against every norm, value and law of our land.'

'First of all, Azhar…' Meera took off her glasses and pretended to clean the lenses with the pallu of her sari. 'Movies and soaps, music and rituals of India are not new to any Pakistani. Have you ever spoken to your parents about India? Or, if you are lucky to have one, you could ask your grandparent? They could tell you more about Indian culture than you could have ever learnt from the movies. You would agree with me when I say, movies are merely a glamourized and hyped-up image of any culture, person or society.' Meera paused to put the glistening glasses back on her face, now quite stern.

'Second, what makes you think that your own culture is so vulnerable that it might get ripped apart just because a certain section of the population watches Indian soaps on TV or Indian movies in the cinema?'

'The youth, Miss Malik, is impressionable,' he said, folding his arms across his chest, thus indicating to her that he wasn't impressed.

'Your youth is your problem, Azhar. Instilling belief in your own roots is your job. Just because you fail at it, don't blame the merchant who is only trying to sell his product.'

'It's not just India, you know...' he began.

Meera was agitated at the persistence since she still had a couple of slides to discuss for her lecture on Bilateral Communication. She almost snapped, 'What, now Thailand is also creating havoc in your household?'

The class laughed but Azhar continued, 'What about the West?'

'Define "the West".'

'America.'

'Only America? And you mean North America, I suppose?'

'No, I mean the Americas, Europe, UK...the West, Miss Malik, they are taking away our values from us.'

'Although I am confident they are doing no such thing, but

for the sake of argument, who do you approve of, then? Asia-minus-India, and Africa? Or maybe, Antarctica alone?'

'I am glad you can take this as a joke, Miss Malik,' Azhar said drily.

'I actually imagine no other way of seeing this. If your youth enjoys a McDonald's burger once a week, that does not mean the mothers at home have stopped cooking daal chawal with achar. If half the girls in your classroom wear skin-tight jeans, do not forget the other half wears hijab. Just because your culture, and, mind you, not your religion but your culture, defines that the ideal place for a woman is to stay "within the four walls", a score of frustrated and bored housewives do get divorced for the sake of living a financially independent life. Why so insecure, Azhar? What is the problem?'

'I am not insecure. You cannot make personal attacks on me in the class.' He was upset.

'There is no personal attack in a head to head, Azhar. I only find it amusing that all you could infer from my arguments was me attacking you, which I was not,' said Meera, standing up from her chair. It was time, and she was pretty upset for having wasted the last few minutes in a discussion that had led neither party anywhere.

'Discussion,' she insisted, 'is different from an argument. A discussion is meant to bounce opinions and facts off each other, while the rationale behind an argument is usually to win. Winning an argument might be gratifying, but it does not achieve anything, especially in a conference room.' That, too, had been an interesting lecture because the students had brought up the discussions-cum-arguments held at popular political talk shows. Most of the doctorate-degree holders had agreed that a debate on such platforms, aired on national TV, never actually helped the audience achieve anything—opinion or education. Azhar, that day, had done the same to the entire class. However, he was not yet done.

'I understand, you have personal benefits from India. Your books get published there, that is why you are so defensive,' said Azhar, taking his own shot at getting personal.

Meera stopped in her tracks but chose to ignore the immature comment. The time for the class was up and even if her students hadn't gotten much material to write in their thesis, she had found a premise for her new book. She walked out of the conference room for PhD students, a privilege the university had allotted to every department. During her walk in the hallway that led her to her own cabin, a student caught up with her and asked her if she could walk with her. Meera nodded with a forced smile.

The student, Zara, was writing her PhD dissertation and Meera was her adviser. Both of them had had continuous duels discussing the 'methodology' and 'theoretical framework', but having passed that stage, they were now at the point where Zara was analysing the data collected, and every other day, she had to catch Miss Malik on the go, to confirm if she was heading the right way. As soon as they both reached the doorway of Meera's cabin, Zara knew she could not trespass her teacher's personal space any more. Thus, she took leave. Meera shut the door behind her and threw her shawl on the visitor's chair. She then fixed her sari, sat in her office chair, slid off the high heels under the desk and relaxed, leaning back.

She was agile and active, and yet, there was no denying the fact that she had aged. The white on her head wasn't the only thing indicating her experience and observations in life, but also the wrinkles on her face, the smile and frown lines, the crow's feet and the heather-coloured bags under the sunken grey eyes—all were pointing towards the late sixties she was pushing through. After making herself a cup of jasmine tea and downing it, she took out her writing pad and loyal fountain pen from the drawer and sat down to write. Thanks to Azhar, she started working on the book during her free time and didn't stop until the next three months. Exactly around the same time when her students submitted their dissertations, Miss Meera Malik was ready with the manuscript of her new book.

༄

The real challenge was to look for a publisher. Although she was a seasoned writer by then, she still remembered the toil and peril she went through the first time she wanted to publish a book. She, at forty-five, went into the dingy old lanes that criss-crossed through the famous Urdu Bazaar like a complex cobweb. The printers and publishers were many, but those who agreed to print a non-fiction book written in English had doubts about its prospects. She was told that she could get a hundred copies published after she paid for the paper, ink and binding. That was not quite acceptable and, hence, she was left with no option but to surf the World Wide Web.

Among the plethora of options she had, one was to look for a literary agent, who, to her surprise, were non-existent in her country. She found a couple of boutique publishers but they turned her down by saying they could not invest in non-fiction, since they only did 'coffee table' books. Meera was quite discouraged by the scene in front of her. Just before she was about to give up, she picked up some of the books penned by her fellow writers in the previous years. How had they gotten it done? One was printed in UK, another in USA, one in Canada... it overwhelmed her. She could submit a proposal but why would a book, based on the similarities, differences and bilateralism of the subcontinent where she resided, be of any interest to a publisher or reader in those countries? She picked up a fourth. It read 'New Delhi, India'. That lit a spark of hope in her heart. She brought down her entire collection of books from the bookshelf that spanned the floor and the ceiling. Much to her joy, she found that half of her non-fiction collection related to Asia, and the subcontinent in particular, had been published in India. The writers were both local and foreign.

∽

What Azhar had thought to be a grand, closing remark for his verbal combat, was a result of her final resort to book publishing. Indian literary circles had accepted her, and, that too, on its own merit and not on basis of her nationality. There were those in her own country who had lauded her work and there were those who tagged her 'unpatriotic'. In any case, Meera was not one for conventional thought. She had learnt to ignore and avoid emotional rhetoric, both nationalistic and cultural.

Luckily, this time she did not have to go through the same turmoil, for she had her reliable literary agent, a resident of Delhi, to take on the book. The idea behind her new book, *Living in a Glocalized world: The myth of Globalization*, was a pun at globalization. She had argued in her book, just like she had done in the conference room at the university, that globalization was a myth.

'While we would be more comfortable in believing that the world is getting smaller with the advent of technology, the fact remains that the physical borders around countries are getting taller and more barbed. The multinational conglomerations are spreading their wings across the globe but, at the same time, they can't do without localizing their staff, budget, product and yield. For an American company to open office in an Asian country, the requirement would begin from understanding its economy and end at meeting the clients' expectations over time. While the franchise could boast of providing jobs to the locals, the truth remains that an Asian country would need far more capital and investment to do the same in America. Thus, the concept of globalization becomes a rather lopsided concept of dominance.'

Meera Malik was a radical. The political economy of the term 'globalization,' failed to impress her in terms of the area of communications, as well. She wrote that communication and media information, too, were not globalized in terms of balance. Global news cannot attract as much audience as local news does. 'A local is not interested in what happens overseas since it does not affect him or her. He also does not care what happens in the country next to his because that, too, does not affect him as much as the price of a commodity in his own country does. For that, his medium of information need not be a high-priced TV channel as he is more comfortable in acquiring the rate for wheat via "word of mouth" from a reliable friend than the "biggest network for global news". Thus, the media's purpose is only limited to serving a handful in developing countries, instead of the masses. Little or no inclusion of masses in the structure of communications hardly means globalization.'

Her book was published across the border and, once again, some right-minded booksellers had refused to stock her book in their stores. She had to go to the customs department of the national airlines, to receive a parcel that contained her share of 'author's books' from overseas. The officials had asked her several questions about the contents of the parcel and the book, as well as the shipping procedure. Until then, it was a normal routine. The sixty-seven-year-old woman had begun to reap the harvest of her hard work when she saw her book sell online and at stalls, but what followed was something new.

The current chairperson of the Political Science department at the varsity had been Meera's student and he arranged for a book launch at the campus. On the day, Meera was standing in a big hall with very little audience—some fellow professors, some family members and a few loyal students who had come to cheer their favourite teacher. She was standing behind the rostrum, at the launch of her book that had been released in India. After her speech, the convener of the stage had informed the audience that Miss Meera Malik had been invited to the

Jaipur Literary Festival in India, to not just launch her book, but also meet up with her fans and speak at a forum by the International Writers' Community.

The applause was huge. Meera Malik was happy with herself and with life. She prepared herself to travel to the country she had heard so much about. Her father had had war stories to share, her students had rants against it and she was among those in the population who wanted to be friends with her neighbours. She did not have a lot of relationships in her life to commit to, so her concerns were more social. Her thoughts were not about the future of her children or her grandchildren, but the future that was collectively affecting everyone she knew.

Meera had applied for a visa to attend the literary festival. A few days after the book launch, someone painted 'traitor' across her cabin's door at the university. She had the door repainted. The following week, she found her car spray-painted with dirty abuse, and there were pictures of her on the noticeboard, wearing a red teeka in the middle of her forehead. She ignored these onslaughts. The news on campus made it to the national media, which aired it and tried their best to get a version from Miss Malik, but she kept her mouth firmly clamped. As the news reached the Internet, some people across the border, too, tried to create a ruckus against the festival managers for inviting a Pakistani to India and felicitating her. A small matter was blown up into a fireball within days.

A week ahead of the festival, Meera had to go to the authorities to enquire about her visa, where she was told that the matter was beyond control, and with the ongoing volley of media abuse from both sides, it would be better if she changed her mind.

The officers at the visa office weren't very flexible. She still pushed the officers for the release of her visa and went home. Optimistic as she was, she prepared a speech for the forum, selected a sari and asked a friend to keep her mini-aquarium for the time she would be gone. She kept pursuing the visa officers until the very last day. However, when that day was over, she sat on her rocking chair with her laptop on her legs, and watched videos, heard forum discussions and read the titles of the newly released books on social media. She had joined the rest of the panel of foreign writers through a live feed to interact with the audience, not worrying what political repurcussions her virtual appearance might create. She watched as many speakers brought up the unnecessary chaos over the book. At the end of the day, she thought to herself, it could have been a delightful weekend. Her new book lay on the table, right in front of her eyes. She stared at the subtitle 'The myth of Globalization' for the longest time and shook her head in dismay just before reaching out to turn off the lamp.

⁓

Meera had a mixed set of emotional experiences during and after the publication of her book. She wanted to write more, and challenge the 'status-quo' ideals of her immediate environment and beyond. Having experienced the sincerity of a very welcoming group of people in India through the virtual world, it had become increasingly desirable for her to diminish the doubts in her people's minds about their neighbour. All her life, she had thought very little about the various kinds of social media, but the they became her only source to cut through a non-porous border, to enjoy a virtual mehfil of sharing the best verses by Mir Taqi Mir and Mirza Ghalib with those people whose language was neither Urdu nor Farsi, and yet, they quoted couplets much better than her.

Meera soon quit her job at the university. Not because she was threatened, but because she had found a new purpose. She stayed the last couple of months teaching and letting her students get done with their PhD dissertation until she let the curtains fall on her teaching career. Meera Malik, a retired professor, single, had begun on a new journey of book writing. It was like getting a new lease of life, professionally.

All her life, Meera had made it a point to categorize and compartmentalize her hours, days and weeks according to the requirement of her career. She had several colleagues, who were married, had kids and had successful careers and she was all praise for their juggling abilities. However, she had set certain standards for her life. She wanted to measure it with how much education she could acquire and impart. Her learning experience had come to a standstill until the idea for the book has struck her, and now, she had to embark on the new path that life had set in front of her.

Meera filled her days with writing. She was happy to have her books showcased at literary festivals, even if she could not herself attend them. A new surge of accomplishment and self-actualization had begun at the age when people are finally wrapping things up. Within three years, working on her fourth book, she received an email from the organizers of a local literary festival, nominating her for 'Best Non-Fiction Writer'. Meera thanked them and set to work again.

A few weeks later, she found herself clad in a sari, speaking to a huge group of people in her beloved Karachi, thanking them for an award she had not expected.

'Writing has been a whirlwind experience for me,' she spoke into the microphone. 'A writer's job becomes increasingly difficult with every new idea that has to be encompassed within a book, since ideas are subjective chunks of personal experiences. In spite of this, the writer is the craftsman who deliberately deletes his or her own opinion and prejudices in order to present a bigger picture to the reader. It is never easy to chuck out subjectivity; never easy, but necessary. However crazy that sounds, an idea, a thought, has to be put out in the open if change is desired. In the end, Mark Twain wins, for telling us centuries ago, "A person with an idea is a crank until the idea succeeds".'

# Eeman
## *Keeping faith*

Sahiba had always wanted sons. But the way fate had it, all five of her pregnancies gave her daughters. It was not like she wasn't happy with the lot she had, but her constant reminders to her daughters about not being sons became the sore point in their hearts from a very young age. In other words, Sahiba was constantly telling her children that they weren't good enough for her.

As the daughters grew up, Sahiba became more and more complaining about not having a 'shoulder' to share the burden of her daughters. Sometimes, during such moments, she would relate to her daughters, the account of each of her pregnancies. She ended every story the same way each time— in the end, it was just a girl. The girls wept with their mother when she talked about her labour pains, or how hard the stitches of a C-section surgery hurt, even without knowing what either felt like. However, they did get familiar with the pain in the years to come, when they gave birth to their own children. One of her daughters, the middle one—Zainab—had three pregnancies. She had had surgeries to give birth. When it was the third time for her to go into labour, it was miraculous. It was a normal birth, but it changed her forever.

Islamabad, the city where Zainab lived with her husband and children, is an artificial city of Pakistan. It began with being nothing but a patch of grassland between the towering Margalla Hills—the foothills that stretch out to the Murree Range and from there they connect to the great Himalayas. It was not until the late 1950s that Field Marshall Ayub Khan, hailing from the picturesque valley of Abbottabad, decided to inhabit the grassland and make it the capital city of Pakistan.

Currently, Islamabad is the prettiest, greenest and most diverse city in the country. Still, when it is said that it is artificial, it means that the people are mostly migrants. They might be millionaires who earn their foreign currency salaries at the bureaucracy or from a small, local business, but their hearts have been left behind in their homelands. Every Eid, twice a year, half of Islamabad is empty. There is almost no worker who is local to the city. They all travel back to their towns and villages for holidays, nearly deserting the roads and emptying the streets.

Zainab's ultrasound for the last trimester was scheduled on one of those days when the commuters had gone back home to mourn the Ashura, during Muharram, and Islamabad had come to a silent halt. The traffic was few and far between. She had been baking that day as it was a school holiday and her older kids, six and three, had both asked for cream-cheese-filled doughnuts. 'With frosting on top,' her younger boy had chirped in his parrot-like voice.

Yes, she had sons. She did not pray for them to be sons when they had squirmed around in her womb. She had just wanted them to be healthy. She was on cloud nine when she held her boys in her arms for the very first time, but she also knew that she wouldn't have felt any less happy if they had been girls. People had wished Zainab good fortune and an army of sons when they saw her swollen feet and rounded belly for the third time. She had found that offending. The level of her annoyance was such that during each of her pregnancies, when the radiologist had asked her whether she would like to know the gender of the baby, she had refused. 'I would rather not know and be surprised with the bundle of joy God would send wrapped under layers of my own blood and flesh,' she swore silently. Both the sons did bring with them a piece of paradise for her and beautified her life like nothing else had.

During the ultrasound her radiologist asked her a new question—whether she would like an amniocentesis to determine the chromosome count of the baby.

She asked him, confused, 'Is that necessary?'

'It isn't, but it will give you an insight.'

'Into what?' She was a little frightened.

'Women get it done as a check for Down's Syndrome.'

Her psychology class from college started running through her brain. She asked the doctor that if such was the case, would the test performed on the amniotic fluid help them treat the foetus inside the womb. He replied in the negative. Zainab took a deep breath, blinked her eyes to regain her composure and swallowed the quiver in her voice.

'Then,' she said with her eyes fixed on his face, 'I would rather not have it.'

She surprised her doctor, and in doing so, she surprised herself as well; such is the valour of a pregnant woman's heart. Listening to Sahiba's laments of not having a son all her childhood, Zainab had wanted to be a boy—her mother's son; a man. However, during those hours of labour that she spent in pain for all three children, her resentment against her own gender disappeared. No man can have the strength, stamina or prowess to nurture another human inside his body for almost a year.

It makes eating, drinking, sleeping, squatting, walking, running errands, sitting and even breathing, harder than ever. Making a baby stretches the skin, brings wrinkles to the face, darkens the skin's pigment, takes away a part of one's youthful beauty, gives a woman cellulite and makes the skin sag. It makes the cervix and ovaries prone to diseases. A woman either becomes obese or weak. She loses blood for over a month. She suffers from sleep apnea. She stays up all night to tend to the newborn and works dutifully all day for the rest of the family, for months at a stretch. A man cannot spend even a day like that, can he? There's a reason why men don't have a womb—they wouldn't be able to handle all this.

Bearing daughters is not a burden on the mother, but a privilege. Every time a woman gives birth to another, she is possibly channelling another mother into the world, another source of God's system to keep the world running. How interesting it is, thought Zainab, that a female foetus develops ovaries and eggs in her body, even before she comes into the world. She is prepared to be a mother even before her own birth. That, and that alone, is reason enough to welcome a girl child, rather than label her a 'single-run' in comparison to a boy child, who is lovingly labelled as a 'sixer' in Pakistan.

Zainab was a computer programmer by profession. She deliberately took up this line of work instead of the more 'female-oriented' jobs because she had wanted to be a 'son', of course. However, it was a higher plan by God that brought her closer to her subordinate, Amjad, in the office and their relationship turned into marriage soon after.

They had both decided to keep the office environment strictly professional when she was his boss. Knowing that it was not an easy feat to perform for most Pakistani men, Zainab generously let Amjad be the boss at home. She didn't ask him to pitch in for the chores. And he never bothered. She didn't need him for housework anyway—she could afford help—she needed him psychologically, despite all the toughness that she wanted to exude, owing to the brainwashing by her mother.

But on that day, during the scan, Zainab had decided one thing—she was on her own. She did not bother to take his opinion on the matter. From that day, she held herself the only one responsible for her children, all the time and forever.

Three months later, she had the contractions. The children were at school but her husband was still at home. He drove Zainab to the hospital and once she was in the Obstetrics and Gynaecology Ward, he went to pick the kids from school and play 'mother' for them. As opposed to the previous two childbirths her body had been through, this one was proving to be harder. The baby, she had been told, had crowned already. This meant that the baby's face had been rubbing against her uterus for days prior to the contractions and that was making the foetus uncomfortable.

After an excruciating labour that lasted seven hours, Zainab saw the littlest baby girl in the doctor's hands. Her vision was cloudy from having been writhing in pain for seven hours at a stretch so she could not see her features very clearly, but Zainab could see that the baby's face was bruised badly. She even bled from some of those bruises. The doctors were mysteriously silent and they took her away after the traditional 'first cuddle' between mother and daughter.

After getting a clean-up and being dressed, Zainab was told to be ready to feed the baby. The new mother was more excited than ever, because by that time, Amjad and their two children had already dropped by to visit the newest member in the family. Her boys were worried when they saw that Mummy had suddenly gotten thin. The white sheets over and under her, made the older one ask, 'Mummy, do you have a brain tumour?' Amjad and Zainab laughed, for they never knew while they lounged around watching *Scrubs* on the cable TV, this is what their kids had picked up from it.

'No, sweetheart, I don't. I just had a baby. Do you want to see her?' she asked her oldest, preening his hair.

He nodded eagerly, and at that instance, Zainab realized

how lucky her baby girl was, for having such an army of loving men around her. Her husband, however, noticed an expression of worry on his wife's face, and stroked her cheek as he asked her if all was well. She couldn't quite tell him that her motherly instincts had sensed something already. However, until the doctors spoke a word, there was no reason to worry him. So she smiled tiredly, and feebly nodded her head. They waited for an hour but the newborn was not brought to visit her family, for she was going through certain tests. Amjad asked the nurse the same question he had asked Zainab but she assured him it was all routine check-up and tomorrow would be a better day to see the baby.

With visiting hours over and the kids gone, Zainab had nothing to do but rest, and wait to hold her baby close to the bosom that was completely full and ready to nurture the dear one. She fretted about the look in the doctor's eyes and the hurry with which the baby was taken away from her. She also worried about the causes behind the delayed meeting between mother and child. Amid all the mental commotion, Zainab, tired from a long labour, drifted off to sleep.

In the middle of the night, Zainab was awoken by the nurse who held the baby in her arms. She sat up with a startle. It was reassuring to finally see her. The mother could see that the baby's face was still swollen but the bruises had healed a little. At least, the bleeding had stopped, which gave her instant relief. Her eyes were tightly shut and she was wailing for milk with her tiny mouth. The nurse asked Zainab to feed her. She sprang at the opportunity, since the wait had already been long enough.

She brought her close to her bosom and let Nature do its thing.

It turned out that the newborn did not know how to suckle. Nature has its training programme for every stage in motherhood and this stage was strictly based on instincts. The baby was unable to suckle on the milk flowing right from the centre of Zainab's heart to the baby's mouth. Her wails grew louder and Zainab could feel her discomfort. The doctor on night shift was called in and she said that until the test results come in, she could not allow formula milk for the infant. Instead, they inserted very thin tubes into her throat and siphoned the mother's milk from a container into it. Zainab didn't understand why they wouldn't allow a feeder.

While her anxiety had returned and her blood pressure was getting higher and higher, the baby stayed in her cot, a few feet away from Zainab, taking her feed in the most unusual manner. The doctor kept watch until she had had two ounces of milk and, then again, Zainab was handed over the baby to help her burp. The tiny burp gave Zainab tingles of joy. She asked the doctor if something was wrong and she briefly replied that the paediatrician would speak to her in the morning.

The next day, the paediatrician told her that the baby had Down's syndrome. It meant she had one extra chromosome in her genetic structure. Zainab was also told that the baby had a hole in her heart. As alarming as it sounded to her, the doctors assured that time will take care of it and there was a high chance that the gap would close on its own. Zainab felt helpless and completely weak at the hands of fate. However, the way she had conditioned herself, she could not succumb to her weaknesses.

Thus, Zainab began a very sturdy relationship with faith. The baby was too young for a surgery so all Zainab had was hope; a strong faith that one miraculous day, her heart will be healthy.

With the doctors satisfied with Zainab's reaction, and her willingness to become the parent of a child with special needs, she was finally given the baby, to be hers, to be cradled and to be loved. It was not easy, but it was what she wanted. She had immediately decided to quit her job. A nanny had been good enough for the other kids but this one needed her mother.

It was harder on the baby whom Zainab chose to name Eeman, which translates as 'faith'. She was only being herself, but she had a lot to learn. Zainab had to learn how to help and support her with her slower muscular development, which meant, apart from other things, a setback in speech ability.

At the age of one, Eeman hadn't yet started speaking and so, her wails were quite difficult to decipher. Zainab wouldn't know what bothered her when she cried—hunger, bowels, cold, heat, colic, or lack of attention. Motherhood is based on instincts, but the work of a mother becomes tougher with a child who has special needs. She was under a lot of pressure; her husband was dejected at their child's condition, though he didn't quite say it. He kept mum and so, the couple could not really share the responsibilities of the child. He was supportive, but he could not understand that it was tough for Zainab to keep up with the growing child who was different from the ones she had had before. Zainab's life had completely altered. She had signed up for online nursing courses that taught her how to deal with a child who had Down's syndrome.

The next year, the speech problem became worse because Eeman could not express anything she felt. The only way for her to communicate was to either cry or laugh. With growing observation and experiences, she started playing with her older siblings, stroking the pet bunny, as well as differentiating between the kind of food she liked and the kind she didn't. Merely crying and laughing was not enough any more.

Zainab contacted a speech therapist and he agreed to take Eeman under his wing. The first thing he did was to ask the mother to make a list of things Eeman asked for in a day, and on an average. She had to think hard to make a list—food, feeder, water, juice, toilet, bed, toys, teddy bear, upstairs, downstairs, car drive, backyard, swing, feeling cold, feeling hot and talking on the phone. Dr Shaikh drew a 7x7 inch index card with the pictures of all these things on it. There were no words to confuse the kid or the mother. That index card went around Eeman's neck and every time she needed something, they both gradually learnt to contact the chart before starting to cry or going into guessing games. That was the first progress they both made—mother and daughter.

When Zainab took Eeman to the physiologist for her bi-annual check-up, she came back home with mixed feelings. The news from her tests and echogram had been so overwhelming that she had come home, busied herself with the chores, completed an assignment for the online course and knelt down silently in prayer. That is when the tears started rolling and she could only thank the Source of her faith for letting the gap in Eeman's heart close, all on its own. Two years of check-ups, hopes and prayers had brought her to the day when the heartbeat of her youngest child was neither tachycardic (overbeating of the heart) nor bradycardic (slower beating of the heart). It had no hum or buzz. The heartbeat was just like any other heartbeat. She tried to recollect, at that moment, how many times had she paid attention to the heartbeat of her older children. Never, to be honest. It's true, when they say, we never fully realize how rich we are until some of the opulence is taken away.

Zainab and her husband had never been thankful for their older children's heartbeats, until now. Zainab understood quite well that all her children were a blessing from above, and she, as a mother, had a duty bigger than just clothing, feeding, sheltering and educating them, and being a parent in the conventional way. She had to be thankful for who they were and how their personalities bloomed with her constant grooming. She had to appreciate how diverse they would become in their choices but still share the same bond of being her and Amjad's children. Love is not in restriction, but in liberation. One may love their pet bird, but keeping it caged does not do it justice. A bird is meant to fly, make nests and hunt for food all day. A bird in a cage is not being allowed to be the way it was created. It is not being allowed to be a bird. It is not even being allowed to be a living entity.

How could one ever claim to love their kids if they can't celebrate their individual personalities? Zainab had learnt to appreciate the unique way the hearts of each of her children beat.

Later in the day, when her kids sat around her, watching an animated movie, punctuated with the squeals of Eeman when she saw little goblins running around on the screen, she made them all lie down for a moment and put her ear against the ribcage of each one of them. She closed her eyes when she heard the rhythm inside their chests. Her heart soared.

Back in their bedroom, Amjad and Zainab wept and embraced each other for the good news regarding Eeman. Zainab said to him, 'Eeman shall have to wear prescription glasses since she has begun on the myopic trail.' Zainab had been wearing glasses for having myopia since the time she was no more than eight years old. Eeman and Zainab settled on a pair of spectacles during their online search. She wanted pink and so they got two hot pink glasses—one each for mother and daughter. The day Eeman wore them with suspenders that helped her balance them on her nose, the mother-daughter exchanged a high five and also took selfies to celebrate their 'twinning' moment.

By this time, Eeman and Zainab had mastered their index-card communication and were on their way to learn sign language. Eeman was growing up like any other kid. She was lively and lithe. She wanted to run with her brothers up and down the house, and wanted to bowl and bat when they played with their friends in the backyard. There was a lot more that she wanted to say than just asking for food, or help with the toilet. She wanted to complain, tease, and tell her side of the story when her brothers complained that she had messed up their homework. They had a verbal language for that, but with Eeman, sign language was the best option.

Zainab and Eeman both joined a language teaching group at the local community centre. Eeman got exposure to children like herself, and although she was quite anti-social in the beginning, Zainab knew the experience would make things easier for both of them. Zainab met up with several mothers who had kids with special needs. Some were autistic, some had cerebral palsy and some had speech impairment. Every woman she met had a new story to tell. Some were educated and some were not. Some had advanced level training in sign language and some were beginners just like her. Some kids even came alone.

The most important thing Zainab learnt at the community centre was to let go of her judgemental side completely. It was none of her business if some kids came alone to learn sign language. If anyone felt so much for a disabled kid, they would be more inclusive in behaviour, not sympathetic. Zainab would encourage Eeman to participate in a group activity with one of those kids with whom no one else wanted to play. Zainab's empathy grew every day.

Eeman and her mother completed the language course within a month. Zainab had also made new friends. Actually, she felt more comfortable with them than she did with her old friends who always had a tinge of sadness on their faces when they saw her with Eeman. She knew they meant well and she felt their sincerity, but the ease with which she could communicate with mothers who had children with special needs, was exhilarating. She could relate to the happiness when either of them shared an achievement as simple as a three-year-old trying to babble along with the cartoons. A child feeling comfortable with their glasses, a child having learnt all the significant gestures of the sign language—these were achievements. They shared these stories, they congratulated each other. They understood and became more compassionate.

On her third birthday, Eeman had again gotten new prescription glasses because her myopia was worsening. Her speech, although, was improving. Zainab's older children and husband, too, had learnt most of the language. Going out with Eeman along with the rest of the family had become easier. She could look at pictures and ask for her own choice of meal. She could point at a certain ride at the playground and tell her parents or elder brothers whether she 'liked', 'disliked', 'was scared of' or 'wanted to repeat' it. Zainab was grateful to Eeman for struggling so bravely. Her tiny little girl became her hero, for her willpower to deny the disability and move forward was stronger than anyone else's she had known.

During her yearly dental check-up when she was three, Eeman gave her the biggest joy ever. As soon as they entered the dentist's office, she greeted the doctor saying, 'Hey, dude!'

She spoke!

She used her tongue and mouth to utter the simplest set of words (something she must have picked from her oldest son). These words seem like pure nectar pouring down her auditory canal and never had Zainab heard anything sweeter. She went from standing straight to kneeling on the floor, hugging and kissing her girl, with the dentist, Dr Aslam, watching and smiling. She took a few days to repeat the words, but she had taken the first step. Her vocal cords had started to open up. All the while that she had been adjusting to other ways of communication, Nature had unfolded her arms and Faith had sent a ray of light right into Zainab's heart through her child's first words. Not 'Mama' or 'Dada,' but 'Hey, dude'. This meant that she was ready to interact with the world. She had incoherent speech in the beginning—but speech nonetheless.

For one more year, Eeman had to rigorously go through speech therapy so that her sounds could be differentiated from each other; the phonics had to be worked on. Zainab and Eeman did it together. They went to the gym together and by the end of the year, Zainab was sitting in the principal's office of the public school, waiting to sign the admission papers for Eeman. She had proven to be a smarter child than most and was capable of sharing a classroom with kids of her age. Zainab realized that Eeman had been such a great teacher to her. She remembered the girl she was, in her mother's house—the one who was angry at herself for being the 'weaker' sex. She had progressed into being brave when she had children swimming around in her womb. And now, she took pride in being a woman and a mother—especially a mother to a child like Eeman, who made her have complete trust on her Faith and on her own being.

# Acknowledgements

Writing a note of thanks is old-fashioned business. Thinking about it brings to mind, images of colourful bouquets which have been carefully picked, handwoven baskets and perfumed cards to be written on. On the other hand, a page of acknowledgement does not allow the liberty to get all romantic and emotional, but, as any logophile would argue, words still help to convey a spurt of emotions; they nestle deep and ring through the readers' minds for a long period of time.

The people to whom my gratitude is due, are my dearest ones.

My father, my hero, who taught me to read, write and observe. I can never thank him enough for being the positive influence that he has been, and continues to be, in my life. My mother, to whom I owe everything that I am today, thank you. Amir, my better half, life partner and soulmate, thank you for completing me emotionally as well as intellectually. This book would not have been possible without you by my side.

I am grateful to Rafia and Shujaat Ali for being my ultimate rocks of support throughout the compilation of this book, as well as ever since I have been alive. Thank you, Bushra, for being so kind and encouraging. To Mrs Yasmin Soofi, a teacher who taught me how to critically read literature and write a good sentence, I shall always be indebted. I hope I can do justice to the words that express my gratitude to Suhail Mathur, the literary agent who believed in my work and, through his glorious agency, The Book Bakers, helped me realize a dream I had nurtured ever since I knew what I wanted to do with my life.

Sanjeev Mathur and his wonderful wife, Kitty Mathur, have been utterly kind with their encouragement and friendship, both of which I cherish. I am indeed grateful to my Commissioning Editor, Shambhu Sahu, for being patient and helpful throughout the process of publication and to the lovely Debangana Banerjee, for toiling over the manuscript and doing her best to turn it into a book. Also, thank you to Rupa Publications for allowing me to get on the bandwagon. It is an institution which I have admired every time I have read one of its great works of fiction.

Lastly, to the angels in my life, my children Mumtaz, Mahnaz and Zara, thank you for brightening up my life and being the apples of my eye. With you by my side, no task remains uphill. Your constant support and belief just adds to my enthusiasm and courage, every single day. You are the purpose of my life.

What a score of people I had to thank, all of whom provided rungs for the ladder to this accomplishment. Thank you folks! You all rock!